What I Learned From Men

A Novel

Jenell Hollett

ISBN: 1477483101
ISBN-13: 9781477483107
Library of Congress Control Number: 2012909406

Acknowledgements

Thank you, Joe, for showing me what it means to have a great marriage. Your belief in my talent and your willingness to let me retire and write while you kept on working has given me this incredible opportunity. I'm grateful to you on so many levels. Your love is amazing and you own my heart.

My cherished friend Charlotte Jordan—thank you for seeing potential when this book was just an embryo. You carved out time to read the early versions and kept encouraging me to publish. Through it all you just said, "Oh honey, it's nothing." Your friendship has enriched my life. I love how we've proven age is immaterial to friendship.

Thanks to my kids Carina and Brent, stepdaughters Claire and Melissa, sons-in-law Roger and Pat, granddaughter Riley, and Riley's dad Luke—I appreciate the joy you bring to my world. There is nothing better than you gathered in the kitchen or around the table, laughing, eating, and talking. Being around you inspires me to write richer characters and family scenes. Carina, when you read the final draft in one sitting, remembered details, picked up on subtleties, and said you liked it—it was an incredible compliment. You rarely read anything besides Vietnam history. Brent, thank you for letting me steal your lines for this book. You have a way with words!

My wonderful mom, Ruth Eli, my family by choice, the Loders, my brother, Bradley Eli, my nieces, Chelsea and Chloe, my "little sis," Julie

Vickers, and my extended Melnechuk, Hollett, and Eli families—there is a security in our family that makes us survivors. We can always count on unconditional love, generosity, and "I'm here for you" which is invaluable and all too rare in this world. Thank you for patterning unconditional love from my very first memories. Thank you, Mom and Jimmie Loder, for giving my manuscript the coveted "Mom's two thumbs-up."

Russ and Michelle Haneline, Jerry and Linda Becker—you are incredible parents who have led your families through life's most difficult times. I'm so grateful to have your example, and to know love, prayer, and friendship will rise above the most challenging circumstances. Thanks, Michelle, for being an early reader and supporter of this book.

Buffy Halvorsen—your professional knowledge and personal friendship were invaluable as I dealt with the intricacies of writing a counselor into this book. Thank you for sharing your expertise and your love of reading with me and thanks for all the times I've just enjoyed being your friend.

Peggy Evart, Dolores Kuhlman, and Jimmie Shoshone—thank you for being my "aunts by choice." The love and wisdom you share make such a difference in my life. Thank you for teaching me the things you've mastered and for encouraging me to listen for God's leading.

Ana Chota, Diana Hoppe, and Sheila Hoyt—at a time when my life was in constant change, you were there with open arms, great food, and lots of laughter. I can never thank you enough for the wonderful times we've shared, for your continual encouragement to improve and explore, and for the love you share so freely with me.

Joe's Friday morning Small Group—thank you for providing a consistent safe place for my husband to talk with other men and for holding him up during the rough years. I am forever grateful for your open hearts when Joe and I married. John and Joy Cooke, your friendship has truly enriched my life these last six years. Frank Whitlock, I regularly benefit from your deep knowledge of cars and your amazing generosity. You are an amazing friend.

Raquel Mercedes, Liese Cornwell, Carin Wasson, my weekly Small Group, my Texas friends, my Escondido and Newport church families, and my Sacred Hearts Retreat Group—thank you for encouraging me to cherish times with friends, to pursue my enjoyment of writing and speaking, to relax in the generosity of my husband, to learn and grow and mature, and to pray with confidence. Thank you, Sharon Leach and MaryAnn Hadley, for seeing the writer in me so many years ago, before I knew she existed. You taught me to weed out the passive tense and to get excited about words in a published form. Preston Beach and Kris Fuentes, thank you for your eagerness and willingness to read the proof copy of this book. Your students are incredibly fortunate to learn from such knowledgeable and caring educators. I value your friendship and I loved your positive feedback.

My amazing wonderful Gordian Group friends—you have added an entirely new dimension of enjoyment and golf appreciation to my life. Thank you for your interest when I mentioned the idea of writing a book. Harry and Bev Mellon, long before it was published you thought this book was possible and exciting. That meant so much to me. Thank you for being such generous and cherished friends.

Peggy Bour and my friends at the gym—your excitement about this book and about exercise inspires me. I hope you notice the narrator feels better when she exercises. Me too! You're the best.

Darren Raymond—what a kick to get your feedback, make strategic changes, and watch the rough edges smooth out into a readable story. Thank you for seeing the holes and helping me fill them. Without you, this book would still be hidden in my computer, longing for a good editor. Bessie Gantt, your editorial skills are incredible and your positive feedback—priceless.

Brooke Austin and Team Two at CreateSpace.com—thank you for everything you've done to make this book come to life. I was impressed from the first phone call. Now I know why authors all over the web rave about you and your company.

And finally, I want to thank the men who have enriched my entire life. You have mentored me, encouraged me, reminded me to be a better person, taught me about vehicles and home repairs and construction, challenged or supported or completely disagreed with my position in meetings, and refused excuses when I was wrong. Because of your honesty, I understand women are not the only ones who experience loneliness, fear, discouragement, and confusion. Because of your caring and kindness, I have survived difficult times. I have been blessed with many wonderful women in my life, and I am grateful to say I have also been blessed by the friendship of many good men.

Thanks to all of you. You are my life's greatest blessing. I thank God for each of you and for the gift of being able to write.

Jenell Hollett

1

I've spent most of my adult life trying to convince my older sister, Jen, that there's a valuable place for male friends in my life. Don't get me wrong—I'm a big fan of more-than-friends, but I keep running into great guys who turn out to be just friends. Jen doesn't buy it.

"We're just not wired that way," she said one afternoon over cappuccino at our favorite Java Jungle. "You're ignoring the facts of gender-related chemistry, especially from a guy's perspective. Charlie says no guy will spend time with a woman he doesn't find attractive."

Charlie is her husband of nine years who, according to my sister, has read every philosopher of merit and is the reigning family genius in intellectual matters. That's her opinion. I think Charlie is irritatingly arrogant and stuck on himself—I've thought so since the day he walked into my mother's kitchen, sat down at our table, and began dominating every family conversation.

"Well," I replied, "I agree with C.S. Lewis. Friendship alone is the most fully human of all loves."

To counteract Charlie's self-proclaimed wisdom and Jen's adoration of it, I sometimes find myself searching through the hard drive of my mind, grasping for something that sounds impressive. This time I extracted a C.S. Lewis quote from *The Four Loves*, a book I was forced to read in high school and might have actually enjoyed in college.

"I just don't agree," Jen said. "Besides, what's the point of a guy friend anyway? Either I want to be with the guy or I don't, and if I want to be

1

with him, clearly there are stronger reasons than talking." She raised one eyebrow. "If I just want to talk, I can talk to you."

"You just don't get my point," I said as we gathered our things and took one last sip before pitching two dollars' worth of coffee into the nearest trash. "It's not about replacing sisters or girlfriends—it's about adding the male viewpoint. I've learned a lot from my guy friends."

"I'll bet you have," she said with a wink as she threw her purse into the passenger seat of her Grand Cherokee. "See you soon."

≪≫

2

My sister and I are about as different as organic juice and triple espresso. Both liquids, but that's where the similarities end.

Our differences were apparent from birth. According to Mom, Jen was the petite baby with the brown eyes and the "let's get it done" attitude—the baby who nursed efficiently, the toddler who organized her dolls by size and hair color.

Jen grew into a statuesque woman with great organizational skills and stunning features: dark eyes, olive skin, and silky chestnut hair. She looks like a tropical beauty and runs her life like a CEO. There's no lounging around the beach with my sister. She's too busy running her event-planning business, efficiently handling the details of family life, and being supermom to the kids she and Charlie produced almost immediately after their wedding.

While my sister is the exotic beauty of the family, I look about as exotic as a tourist. My hair is dark, but the rest of my natural coloring should rightly belong to a redhead—light complexion, green eyes, and freckles. Our family's gene pool obviously contains water from many continents.

For the last few years, I've been an executive assistant by day and a master's degree student by night. Unlike my sister, I prefer the scenic route to a goal. To hear Mom tell it, I had to be coaxed into nursing because I was far too interested in the texture of Mom's blouse or the pictures on the wall. Don't get me wrong, I still have goals and I do a very good job reaching them, but I enjoy the trip as much as the destination.

Although Jen is five years older, she and I never had any problems spanning the age gap. Somehow we always found common interests and thrived on each other's attention. In elementary school, she'd wave out the sixth-grade window as I walked toward first grade. At home, we'd play games on the living room floor and soccer in the backyard. No one ever convinced Jen she was too big or too cool to play with me.

I worried a little when she entered high school. It seemed the perfect opportunity to dump the big sister/little sister routine. But Jen defied the norm and kept making time for me. She'd let me help her study for history tests and try on different shades of her lipgloss. During her senior year of high school, Jen would pick me up at school and tell me to keep an eye out for Bobby Longman. Sometimes we'd circle the block three times giggling until he happened to walk by.

Jen and I were both smart-mouths in high school, girls who survive through verbal comebacks designed to keep male egos on constant alert. Although we didn't attend high school at the same time, Jen cleared the trail for me by providing make-up tips, the inside scoop about teachers, and creative ways around the rules. I watched and learned as she carefully picked her way through the landmines of high school dating. Often in the evenings after she returned from a date, we'd sit on her bed giggling together, deciding if she should dump this guy or just freak him out by talking about emotions.

Even though Jen's now married with children, we've stayed amazingly close. Sure, our adult opinions have typically been diverse, as diverse as our looks. Jen has always viewed life in defined terms; I see a spectrum of options. We challenge each other, tossing around concepts that expand into fascinating conversations. Whether we agree or disagree, our discussions are never boring, and, amazingly, we always walk away loving each other more.

"The male viewpoint on life intrigues me," I told Jen during a quick lunch near my work. "They look at life differently than we do."

"Well, that's a shock," she said sarcastically.

"Don't blow it off just because you don't understand it," I persisted. "Just the other day I had a really interesting conversation with Max about the reasons people date. Unlike you, Max thinks there are many reasons people date."

"Oh come on," she said, her exotic eyes squinting my direction. "We all date for the same reasons…to avoid loneliness, to find the ethereal soul mate, to practice the marvelous techniques that guarantee the continuation of our species."

"Why must every conversation with you end in the topic of sex?" I said in mock-Puritanical horror. "Max said men date for hundreds of reasons, some selfish, some internally driven from beyond their conscious mind."

"Such as…?" she prodded.

"Well, he thinks it depends on the stage of life the man is in—whether he's in a transient stage or a settling-down stage. In other words, whether he's looking for adventure or someone to build a life with. If a man is in the transient stage of life, Max says it's pointless to try to domesticate him. The timing is all wrong."

"Well, Max should know," Jen said without attempting to mask her cynicism. "He's managed to stay in the transient stage well into his thirties and avoid all the unnecessary baggage of a wife, kids, house payments, and responsibility."

"Don't be quite so hard on him," I countered. "Although he's definitely not the most familial guy I know, at least he admits he's not ready."

"He never will be, as long as he has you to talk with and someone else to sleep with," Jen said with a downturn in her voice. "You're going to spend your life being best buddies with all these guys while they remain transient."

My sister has a way of hitting hard even when she doesn't mean to.

I thought about her words for a long time, especially late at night when the sheets were cold and my feet wouldn't warm up.

≪ ≫

3

"Hey Max, it's me. Call me when you have a minute."

I try not to leave long messages on Max's voicemail. He's a little anal about long messages and he let me know after I left three or four. He called me back an hour later with an immediate reference to the long and boring meeting he'd just endured.

"Let's go get some food tonight," I ventured. "Sounds like you need something to do besides sit in boring meetings, and I miss talking with you."

"Want to go to that Chinese grill?" he asked.

"That sounds great," I said. "I like an intriguing discussion over stir fry."

Mandarin House Grill was packed with families. Apparently kids really enjoy watching vegetables and meat sizzle on the flat round grill because they were making high-pitched noises and running back and forth from the tables to the grill where the chef stood intently, purposefully ignoring them.

"If I'd wanted this much noise, I'd have gone to my sister's house," I joked.

Max smiled. He tolerated noise well and even enjoyed other people's children in small, carefully controlled doses.

"Remember when we talked before about why people date and the phases of life?" I asked.

"Yeah," Max said as he grabbed a piece of chicken with his chopsticks. "I remember."

"Well, I wondered if there are men, like you for instance, who never move out of the transient phase?"

Max stopped mid-chew and looked directly into my eyes. He looked cautious and cynical, like a man who knew there was more to the question than the sum of the words spoken.

"Where'd that come from?"

"It's just a question," I said. "Don't read too much into it. I'm just curious."

It was the truth. I was curious. My sister had forced the question into my mind, and it seemed perfectly reasonable to ask a man for the answer rather than asking a bunch of women who could only conjecture and theorize.

"Well, I guess there are men like that. But I don't think I'm one of them," Max said as he resumed chewing. "I still think there'll come a time when I'm ready to settle down with the right woman and live the domestic life. Just not yet." Max paused. "I think a lot of men are careful enough to wait for the right person and the right time."

I looked at Max as he chewed. Athletic body, nice face, financially comfortable, plenty of dating opportunities. If there were such a thing as a right time, he should have encountered it by now.

"What if there isn't a right time?" I asked.

"That's a distinct possibility," Max said.

"Yeah," I said. "Maybe for some guys the benefits aren't enough to offset the difficulty of responsibility, house payments, and college funds."

"Maybe."

Max had moved from thinking to simply agreeing—a bad sign. I learned this from him a long time ago. When he was on unfamiliar conversational turf, he'd say very little and stay low like a soldier hunkering down before a firefight.

"Max, I'm not trying to pin you down. I just don't understand how guys like you don't feel the need to find a great woman and spend your life with her."

"Who said I don't feel that need?" Max glanced at the family two tables away.

"So do you?"

"Yeah, sometimes," he said. "Sometimes I think about what it would be like to have a family—a great wife and kids."

8

He paused, glanced around the room again, then spoke slowly as if the thoughts were buried and required considerable time to surface.

"Here's the problem…I can't create her," he said in a tone that reminded me of an attorney presenting his closing arguments to the jury. "I have to find her. And so far I haven't." He stopped looking around the room and stared at the soy sauce.

"Hey, have you noticed the new construction on Fourth Street?" he asked. The subject change was swift. We both pretended it was smooth.

"Yeah, I did notice that," I responded. "Any idea what's happening there?"

And just like that, our deep conversation was over. I decided not to push it. I've learned that from Max. He can converse effortlessly and at length on a wide range of topics, but he can only deal with small doses of introspection. It must be a scary place inside his head because he rarely ventures in and he won't stay for long.

≪ ≫

4

"I think I've figured you out," my sister said as we drove to pick up her daughter Sophie at kindergarten. I'd taken the day off to write a paper, and after two hours of writing I called my sister and abandoned my computer.

"Figured me out in what way?" I asked.

"I think you keep guy friends around for protection." She glanced in her rearview mirror and then slyly tilted her head toward me.

"Protection?" I said with a startled laugh. "And just how do you figure that?"

"Well, first, if you need an escort or a dinner companion, one of your guy friends will suffice. Second, it allows you to convince yourself you have all the men you need in your life. And third, these guys give you enough attention to make you feel attractive while you're still free and available if Mr. Right happens along. Your guy friends give you a rather interesting form of feminine protection."

"Who says I need protection?" I shot back, then rolled my eyes as I realized her pun.

"Maybe you don't, but I stand by my hypothesis. Until your Mr. Right shows up, you still have a few someones as a safety net for your femininity. You get the attention and companionship you need to feel attractive. They keep your ego above the fault line."

"Oh brother." I shook my head. "You could get millions in grant money for that theory. It rates right up there with research on bovine flatulence."

My sister pulled up to the school loading zone, got out, and went in to get her kindergartener. When Jen and Sophie appeared, they were smiling and holding hands. Sophie climbed into the back seat and showed us the picture she had colored. She began reciting her ABC's as my sister headed out of the parking lot. I began thinking about all the reasons men were not my safety net.

My mind was debating with itself. I don't need an emotional safety net; I'm a woman of the twenty-first century who is perfectly capable of financial independence, healthy self-esteem, and setting my own goals; I'm capable of looking in the mirror and liking or changing what I see; I'm capable of being friends with guys without using them for my own ulterior motives and pathetic needs.

I thought about the safety net concept so much that my paper suffered. I turned it in, but it clearly wasn't my best work.

≪ ≫

5

I'm not sure when I realized I had to take care of things myself. Somewhere between the time I left home and the day I paid off my car, I stopped depending on my dad to fix everything for me.

Now that I think about it, my sister had a hand in it. One day she just said, "You've got to quit expecting Dad to do all your repair work. He has a house of his own. Fix some of your own stuff."

I know it sounds childish, but the thought that I should figure out how to open a clogged drain or hang a heavy picture using screws instead of nails had never occurred to me. Dad was too parental to tell me and I was too pampered to consider it. But once again, my sister introduced an idea I couldn't dodge.

At the time I was in college and a guy named Bret lived in the apartment below me. He always said I was the best "top person" he'd ever known, which was either a nice compliment or his way of saying I must have a very boring life because there was never any loud noise. Bret had dark hair and was relatively handsome. He had a variety of hobbies, evidenced by the equipment that over-populated his limited space. A ski boat took up most of his garage, and his patio always had a surfboard, a guitar, or some rollerblading equipment near the portable barbecue. Conversations with him were easy and diverse, and they always ended with me smiling as I walked up the steps to my apartment. He would normally have been exactly my type, but for some inexplicable reason there was a notable lack of chemistry between us. It was the perfect set-up for a friendship, and we both instinctively knew it. So sometimes, late at night, if I saw him alone on his patio or he saw me start to climb the steps, we'd talk.

Bret was the one who clued me into the idea that when something is wrong or needs to be fixed, noises can tell you things. Don't laugh. I didn't know that because I'd never had to listen before. Dad always took care of it before I had to analyze it. Bret told me the noises I heard in the pipes of our apartment building were no big deal, just air in the lines—perfectly harmless. But if I ever heard my toilet making gurgling sounds that could be serious. Who knew? One day I was driving home from school, and I heard what sounded like someone hitting the side of my car with a hammer. Fortunately, Bret was outside shaking sand out of a blanket when I drove up.

"Hey," I said casually. "Should I be worried if my car has a banging sound?"

Now I have to admit, I expected a simple response like yes or no, but instead Bret started asking all these weird questions.

"Is it a sharp ping or a dull bang?"

"I'm not sure."

"Does it get worse when you accelerate?"

"I don't think so."

"Do you hear it more on one side?"

"I can't tell."

"Does it happen when you're going straight or when you turn?"

"When I turn."

My immediate answer surprised us both.

"Really? Just when you turn?" he asked.

"Yes, I'm pretty sure it's loudest when I turn right," I said confidently. That was easy to remember because there are five right turns and only one left turn between my last class and my apartment. Seemed like it was banging whenever I turned.

"Well, it's probably a front wheel bearing," he said.

When I took it in to the shop, the mechanic confirmed it was the right front wheel bearing.

That's what I learned from Bret. Listen to the noises. They'll tell you things. So now I listen to the specific sound, and I try to see if the noise is worse when I accelerate. At least that way I can tell mechanics, "It seems to remain the same whether I accelerate or decelerate," and I tell myself it will make them think twice about overcharging me.

I also learned there's no rhyme or reason to male-female chemistry. I still can't believe I wasn't attracted to Bret, but if there was attraction, it wasn't strong enough to overcome the "let's just talk" pattern we had already perfected. Once he told me I had beautiful eyes and he enjoyed watching my expressions when we talked, but he never asked me out or made any moves. He started dating a girl we both knew, and a few months later she moved in with him. Eventually I earned my B.A. and moved, and we lost touch. But I've never forgotten the lesson Bret taught me—to listen to sounds.

First, he showed me that listening is important. I stopped pretending my car never made noises and would always run. Second, he taught me to identify whether a noise was something that required even more careful listening and prompt action or was simply a noise of relative non-importance.

≪ ≫

6

My sister's at it again. Every year or so, she makes it her personal mission to redesign me. Since, in her mind, Charlie is the yardstick by which all good men are judged and since Charlie and I would be a horrible mismatch, in her mind it logically follows that something must be wrong with me and she needs to fix it.

I think my sister secretly fears I'll never meet Mr. Right, resort to meeting men in chat rooms, and end up marrying a child molester. That thought drives Jen crazy, and her compulsive behavior on my behalf drives me crazy.

Jen started these redesign phases when I entered high school. At the time, I didn't mind much. She was successfully immersed in college dating. I was just emerging from the hell of junior high inferiority, and the strong scent of "help me" lingered as if I'd dabbed on *L'Essence de Pathétique*. At times, when I would torture myself with clothing choices, Jen would kindly and casually suggest I wear a particular pair of jeans or my black boots. I encouraged her suggestions, which unfortunately bred the belief they would always be welcomed.

Next she started buying clothes for me, recommending I steer toward certain colors and cuts that coincidentally always resembled her clothes. I knew she wasn't being mean, just sisterly, so I accepted her gifts graciously and relegated most of them to the back of my closet.

After she met Charlie, her suggestions became directives that began sucking the air out of my self-confidence. She was on the path to a good marriage, and I wasn't. By default, that made her the expert, and her words took on a sharp edge. Whether they were actually spoken pointedly or simply received by tender ears really didn't matter. I got tired of listening.

During one of these encounters, I reacted strongly to Jen's suggestion, and she left my room mumbling, "Fine, do it your way. But you can't expect men to find that attractive." It was our low point, and it hurt us both. I was determined to avoid another such confrontation.

So now when Jen begins to show signs of another redesign phase, I leave town whenever possible. Put a little distance between my sister and me, and we miraculously return to normal after about a week. I can't explain it, but I know it works.

A girlfriend of mine suggested Palm Springs, the land of sunshine, poolside relaxation, and very few reasons for my sister to pack up her kids and join us. Perfect.

Cyndi, Leslee, and I sat beside the pool on Friday morning, glancing seductively at the rare young single straight guy who came along every few hours. There was lots of time to think, reapply sunscreen, and read fluff magazines. Like all good girlfriends, we'd each brought four or five magazines, so the pile was large and there was plenty of sex and fashion advice to keep us occupied for days.

The idea of my sister trying to fix me still swirled around the back of my brain, and it irritated me. After all, if your own sister thinks you need changing, how can you deny the reality? Maybe I did need to become someone different. Maybe I wasn't pretty enough or clever enough or talented enough to attract a quality guy. I remembered one boyfriend who was constantly trying to mold me into his vision of the perfect woman. He thought he was subtle. I thought he was controlling, arrogant, and blind. We had some very brutal talks that solved nothing.

"Have you ever dated someone who tried to change you?" I asked Cyndi as she reached for a sip of her margarita.

"Of course," she replied with rolling eyes. "Who hasn't?"

"I haven't," Leslee said, pushing her hat brim up out of her face and looking at both of us. Cyndi and I were incredulous.

"You're kidding, right?" Cyndi said.

"No, I'm not kidding. I don't think any of the guys I've dated have tried to change me."

"Well, that could be because you dated Marc all through high school and your freshman year of college, and then you didn't date anyone seriously for a couple of years after that," Cyndi said, trying to make sense of Leslee's comment. Cyndi and I saw a number of traits in Leslee that could use some serious work; so, frankly, her comment really didn't make sense.

"What made you ask that?" Cyndi looked at me over the top of her sunglasses, her eyebrows raised. "Your sister at it again?"

"Of course," I answered. "She'll keep bringing it up until I walk down the aisle, and then she'll start badgering me about kids."

We all rolled our eyes then went back to reading. I don't know why—the day was beautiful, the mood relaxed—but I couldn't concentrate on the latest gossip or the newest fashion. I wanted to embrace contentment and relaxation, but they were elusive.

I glanced across the pool and noticed a couple as they walked hand in hand. He was on the downhill side of fifty, graying hair and more than a few lines in his forehead. His golf shirt was neatly tucked in and the slightest hint of belly peeked out over his belt. It wasn't a lot of belly, certainly not large enough to be offensive, but it was an embryonic harbinger. It struck me that although he was probably as old as my father, he still looked very good. Most women of any age would classify him as handsome.

The woman beside him may have been stunning at one time, but that would have been years ago. She had all the accessories of a stylish woman—the sunglasses, lipstick, jewelry, and fashionable purse. Maybe at one time she'd had a stylish figure, but it was now well hidden in the softness of a Rubenesque model. Don't get me wrong. I don't believe women should look like popsicle sticks with breasts. Women should have curves. But these were well-padded curves that had melded into pillows around her middle and broadened her backside to a large amorphous mass. You might describe her figure as matronly, if you were feeling particularly kind.

Cyndi poked me and motioned toward the couple with a slight nod which she mistakenly believed was inconspicuous. I nodded back. I'd seen them, and I was pretty sure she was thinking exactly what I was thinking.

Okay, before you go judging me for being so judgmental, admit it, you've done the same thing. Maybe in a different city with a different couple, but you've done it haven't you? You've looked at a couple and mentally said, "Wonder what she sees in him?" or "Wonder what he sees in her?" And ninety nine percent of the time, it's because of physical appearance. So just put your judgment of me back in the drawer. At least I'm admitting I thought it.

So Cyndi and I kept looking, which of course made Leslee curious. Now all three of us were watching this man and his wife walk through the pool area.

"I don't get it." Cyndi finally broke the silence. "Here we are, three gorgeous unattached women in our bikinis spending the weekend without the company of men. And there she is, all one hundred and eighty pounds of her, walking hand in hand with a great-looking man. There's no justice."

"Oh honey, come on," Leslee sighed. "It's not all about looks. We all know that. Besides, if you saw their wedding picture, I'll bet they were a nice-looking couple."

"That was then—this is now," Cyndi said abruptly. She picked up her *Cosmo* magazine and began leafing through the pages.

As the couple moved out of view, I looked across the pool area onto the tenth hole green of the golf course. Two men and two women were playing the round, and all four looked to be well into their sixties. There wasn't a great body among them, but there was a chemistry you could feel across the distance. I kept watching. One man putted in and then held the flag as the two women finished their final strokes. The woman in pink walked over and stood beside the other man, and to my amazement, he gently patted her butt. Right there on the golf course with no embarrassment or fear, he claimed her as his woman by patting her rather oversized, generally flabby, and definitely dimpled butt.

I smiled to myself. You can't help but smile when you see an older couple express affection—just like you can't help but smile when you see puppies or kittens. They're all just so cute. They make you feel hopeful for the future, especially if you hope that little old couple will be you. That you'll be the one playing golf and getting your butt patted instead of drooling and watching re-runs of *The Price Is Right*.

"Hey, listen to this," Leslee said, as she looked up from deep within the pages of her magazine. "Talk about appropriate reading considering the couple that just walked by the pool."

Leslee started reading aloud from an advice column on page eighty-nine. I knew the column. A guy gives advice to women, ostensibly so we can get the male viewpoint on life. About half the time, I could swear it was written by a woman.

Question: I have a womanly ass and wide hips, and I have cellulite on my thighs, even though I'm only in my twenties. It's super embarrassing. I would prefer the lights off when I'm naked, but my man loves my body. Don't men notice cellulite?

Answer: I think if a man loves you, he LOVES you. It's not just your body but the whole package. When he fell in love with you, I'm sure he was attracted to a confident and talented woman. Great guys are the same as great women in that regard. They love you for who you are more than how you look.

Now, someone who loves you may express concerns about your health if you are overweight. They'll probably notice the cellulite and wrinkles as you get older, but I guarantee they won't notice them as much as you do. Will they stop loving you for those things? NO! I've never heard of one person who REALLY loved their partner and then left them because they had a bit of cellulite or flab! Relax, have fun, and love the body you've been given. Clearly your man does.

"Read that again," I said as soon as she finished.

"Sure."

The second reading was even more interesting to me than the first, especially the part about men not noticing cellulite. I started thinking about all the times I'd seen pictures of myself in a bikini and couldn't stop thinking about ways to improve my very slightly bumpy thighs. Not once, never even once, had any of my boyfriends said anything about cellulite to me. In fact, the nice ones always told me they loved me in a bikini.

I'd always assumed they knew better than to say the word *cellulite* to any woman who could grip a sharp object. But now, as I considered the couple by the pool and the foursome on the golf course, I began to think it was because men are blind.

My mind played with that concept for a while.

Men in love = blind to women's flaws

It was an interesting equation, but somehow it didn't balance.

After the trip, during which Leslee and Cyndi and I all absorbed too much sun, drank too many margaritas, and talked too much about old

21

boyfriends, I decided to get Max's perspective on the question of men and their blindness.

We met for drinks at a place called The Stadium Grill. There was plenty of background noise, which was high on my list of restaurant criteria for the evening. I really didn't want to share this conversation with anyone in the next booth.

"Max, I've got a question for you." I launched right into the subject as soon as we'd ordered. "I've heard guys say horrible things about their wives gaining weight. I've seen them leer at the *Sports Illustrated* swimsuit models. I know guys are visual animals. But you should have seen these two couples in Palm Springs last weekend. The men were crazy in love with cellulite-covered women."

I could tell Max was listening even though a large-screen TV just behind my head grabbed his attention now and then. It's a guy thing, I think: ears in one place, eyes in another.

"It baffles me," I continued. "Whenever I listen to ads or read magazines, there are a million commercials for skin creams and beauty products all based on the idea that women have to stay beautiful for their men or the men will leave."

Max rolled his eyes. "You really believe that crap?" he asked. "You know it's all marketing, designed to get you to spend your money on the product du jour."

"Yeah, I know, but isn't there a little truth to that? Don't men notice if we let ourselves go? Are they really that blind when they're in love?"

"Blind, no," Max said emphatically. "Especially at the beginning. We're visual creatures during that initial attraction stage. But something happens when we fall deeply, crazy in love."

"Are you speaking from personal experience?" I asked, trying not to appear too curious. I'd never heard Max talk about being deeply, crazy in love.

"Yes," he answered matter-of-factly, with the tiniest hint of defensiveness. "Just because I don't talk about past relationships doesn't mean I haven't had any. I was deeply in love with someone…" He paused, distracted by a closely-held memory. "It just didn't work out."

"So," I said gently. "You knew she wasn't perfect, and it didn't matter?"

Max sat quietly for a moment. "When I loved her it didn't." He paused. His voice was a little quieter when he spoke again.

"I don't know," he said, moving a piece of broccoli around on his plate and mentally regrouping. "I guess eventually guys realize love is about more than bra size and hair color."

"Yeah, I get that," I said. I took the hint and moved the conversation even farther away from his personal experience and deeper into the third person. "I don't think it would matter to my dad if my mom gained thirty pounds. He'd love her anyway."

"Probably," Max said, as he made eye contact again. "Because they have this life together that's built on so much more than how she looks."

"Okay, I get that," I said. "But what about all the times I've heard guys complaining about their wife putting on a few pounds? What about when guys talk among themselves and make it sound like they'd give anything to run off with the big-boobed beauty in *Playboy*?"

"Some guys will say all kinds of things to look macho and save face," Max said. "Guys are jerks sometimes. But in his heart, a man loves his wife or girlfriend for so many reasons besides her outward appearance. Think of it—as a couple they've probably been through a lot together. Unless their sex life is trashed or they can't trust each other or they're fighting all the time, there's so much more to a relationship than just looks.

"And you have to understand, when a guy really loves a woman, he can't imagine his life without her. Even if she isn't the most beautiful woman in the world anymore, she's still the woman who captured his heart."

"I want to capture someone's heart like that," I told Max. "I want that kind of love—the kind where when my butt is big and flabby, he'll still pat it in public."

Max smiled. "Yeah," he said. "Me too."

Sometimes I wonder if my sister believes I'm capable of attracting that kind of love. I'll probably never know for sure, because my sister may be a lot of things, but she's not cruel enough to say that straight up to my face.

Jen believes her marriage to Charlie is so close to perfect they'll be that couple when they're sixty. I hope she's right, 'cause in my opinion, life doesn't get much better than that. To know your man will love you no matter what—that's good stuff.

≪ ≫

7

I consider myself a reasonably intelligent woman. I know a dead end when I see one. But I'm loath to admit I nearly had an affair with a married man. Some of the things I've learned from men were easy lessons with compact learning curves. Some lessons were harder. This lesson was brutal not because of the fallout, but because I've never quite forgiven myself for being so stupid after age sixteen. Hormones and emotions don't usually rule me, but this time emotion hijacked my brain, and logic sat idly drinking margaritas by the pool.

It all started innocently enough, as most hard lessons do. Joel came in to see my boss one morning, and the chemistry was instant. I was casually dating at the time, wishing I could find someone special but not sure how to do that without seeming desperate. After all, once a woman is old enough to have a biological clock men become hypersensitive, watching to see if there's any evidence of time running out.

Joel had a great smile and a hint of a receding hairline, which I personally have always found attractive. He was tall, well over six feet, with broad shoulders and well-defined muscles pushing against his chocolate brown shirt. I had an instant feeling of surging pheromones—a visceral biologic response I struggled to control.

"I didn't expect to see such a beautiful woman when I walked in," he said before identifying himself. His voice was smooth, his lines practiced. Coming from most men, that line would have been a monumental turn-off, but I was feeling a little unappreciated by men in general, so Joel's words fell on very receptive ears. I wanted to hear how beautiful I was and why men found me irresistible.

"Would you like something to drink?" I asked as he waited for my boss to finish a phone call.

"I'd love a Coke," he replied with some serious eye contact. "Although I'm sure I'd enjoy anything you have to offer."

By then the room was so fogged with chemistry, he could have recited the Pledge of Allegiance, and it would have seemed rich with innuendo.

Joel and I talked for ten minutes as he waited. I leaned in a little too often; he let his eyes wander a little too much. I found myself anticipating the end of his meeting with my boss just so I could see him again.

"I'm already looking forward to the next meeting in a couple of weeks," he said as he left. There was no denying the tingle. I made a mental note to wear my sexy pencil skirt the next time I saw his name on the calendar.

I thought about Joel for the rest of the day. Even though logic told me part of his job was to be charming and friendly, I've always had a fatal flaw—optimism about people's motives. I should have learned the brutal truth in kindergarten. Everyone who acts like your friend might just be after your Hostess Twinkies. Joel was definitely eyeing my Twinkies for all the wrong reasons. I saw his wedding ring. For a few weeks I ignored it.

We met for drinks one day and called it a business meeting. It took Joel about fifteen minutes to make his first move and start exploring the space between my knee and the hem of my skirt with his left hand. A few minutes later, I let Joel kiss me. I considered the pleasures of more kisses. Then, from the depths of my brain, a thought surfaced. I couldn't shake it, so I grabbed my purse and headed to the bathroom to think about it without distraction.

"Guys let you know who they are at the beginning. Believe them."

These words, uttered in high school behind the stadium by my friend Andrew, were as clear in my memory as the day he'd spoken them. Andrew had been consoling me, as he often did, when I had set my sights on another guy of questionable value.

Somehow I'd managed to fall in love, or lust perhaps, with the captain of the football team who looked so good in his uniform but treated women like disposable forks. He'd caught my attention right after I'd been burned by the guy on the back row of chemistry class who was failing every class but looked so good on his silver motorcycle. Which, of course, was right after I admitted my crush on the college guy who was cheating on his girl-friend with one of my classmates. I could really pick 'em.

Andrew had tried to warn me about each of these guys before I did anything to humiliate myself, but I kept telling Andrew he was a pessimist who only saw the worst in people. I kept repeating how important it was to see the good in everyone and how all these guys needed was a woman who really understood and loved them. Andrew would roll his eyes and we'd drive away in his little Honda Civic to get a burger.

One day, Andrew got tired of this routine. He looked me straight in the eye. "You just don't get it," he said slowly, as though I couldn't or wouldn't understand. "These guys will never treat you right. They're jerks. They might as well have it written all over their shirts, 'Date me and I'll treat you like dirt.'"

I just stared at Andrew. I didn't know what to say. He was being so direct, so harsh, so unlike the Andrew who usually protected me and talked me gently back from my tears.

"You have to understand," he continued. "Men tell you exactly who they are at the beginning. Believe them. They're not going to change."

"But," I started.

"But nothing," he said. "They're not going to change."

And for some strange reason, the words stuck. They made sense. I stopped believing the female fantasy that with beauty and intelligence I could inspire a self-centered jerk to suddenly and miraculously treat me like treasure.

I let go of the fantasy and looked across the table at the only guy in high school who had every truly believed I was something special. The music should have hit a crescendo right then, and we should have shared a long passionate kiss. But actually, Andrew and I never dated. We were great friends who just kept being great friends because for us, conversation was more intimate than kissing. I eventually started taking his advice more seriously and stopped selling myself short by choosing guys who were only after my Twinkies, if they noticed me at all.

So there in the bathroom, I took a few minutes to remember Andrew and his sage words. Then I mentally compared Joel-married-guy-at-the-bar with those guys Andrew had warned me about in high school. The com-parison was unmistakable. Joel was a Twinkie-stealer.

I walked out of the bathroom, said goodnight to Joel, and drove home. Joel had told me who he was the first time he walked into my office. In spite of the chemistry that still swirled around us, I was finally wise enough to listen.

≪ ≫

8

It was clear to me something wasn't right between Jenny and Charlie, but I wasn't sure whether to ask or wait for her to confirm my sister intuition. I could feel she was tense when I asked about Charlie, and her answers were more carefully crafted than usual, as if she were creating a very precise novel rather than simply relaying the facts. It wasn't like my sister to hide things from me, but it also was completely like her to leave out details that made her life look somehow out of control. Today the roar of her silence was so loud I couldn't ignore it.

"Jen, is something going on between you and Charlie?"

She jerked her head in my direction with a look that showed she was both puzzled and scared. Obviously I'm not a parent, but I recognized the "hands in the cookie jar" look, and it made my breathing faster.

"Is it that obvious?" she replied, her forehead a mass of question marks.

"Hey, I'm your sister. I know everything, sometimes before it happens to you," I joked. Her expression didn't change in the way I expected; instead her face morphed from questions to sadness.

"I don't know..." her voice trailed off. "I can't put my finger on it, but it feels like Charlie is a hundred miles away." Her expression was as flat and dull as concrete, but she suddenly brightened a little, looked directly at me, and said, "Oh, it's probably just all the stress he's dealing with right now. He's traveling a lot for work and the construction business looks like it's about to enter one of those ten-year down cycles anytime. When you depend on new construction for your living, it must be stressful."

My sister has a lot of talents, but hiding fear and concern isn't one of them. Her explanation was a weak argument, and she and I both knew it. Charlie rides stress like surfers ride waves. He rides it with every muscle finely tuned and walks to his car at the end of the day with his laptop under his arm as though he's just ridden North Shore. Charlie has captured an aura of success and controlled superiority, and it lives inside him without any guilt. I have to admit sometimes I'm envious, but not enough to become anything like him. I've always suspected there's something hidden under that veneer of arrogance and superiority.

"I guess we all have stress," I said, just to keep the conversation going.

"Umm," was her only reply. The silence screamed for an explanation, but neither one of us had one.

<< >>

9

I started wondering whether men had an internal "minimum standard" meter when I was in high school. They were pretty good at hiding it, so frankly it was hard to confirm the thing actually existed until one day, well into my twenties, the guy at the sub sandwich shop openly talked about it.

Now I'll grant you, the sub shop guy isn't usually the best source of information. You get the impression he'd say anything to draw female attention. But this time, all I wanted was confirmation of a fact I already suspected. As long as my source was male and willing to spill his secrets, it was good enough for me.

Most of my Ancient Civilizations class ate at the sub shop periodically, so it was no surprise when, just as I was ordering my grilled chicken with no pickles and no onions, the cute guy on the fifth row walked in with his girlfriend. At least I assumed it was his girlfriend because they had their hands in each other's back pockets, and that's usually a pretty good sign it's not a first date. They looked over the posted menu board, gazed into each other's eyes as they discussed the pros and cons of salami over bacon, and then he must have said something very clever because she burst out in the most irritating laugh I've ever heard. I was watching the sub guy carefully putting mustard on my sandwich. He was watching the cute guy's girlfriend, and, I swear, when she laughed he nearly poured mustard on his hand. His face said it all, but he punctuated the grimace with a whispered comment to me: "Whoa…that laugh puts her under my minimum standard."

So there! It's out in the open now—guys have a minimum standard for women. It was time to do a little demographic research. I started to subtly query guys around campus. It only took a couple of days to confirm everything I'd thought and more.

It also confirmed something else I'd long suspected. Guys buy different mirrors than women. It's the only explanation for the total geek who emphatically stated he wouldn't date any woman with dark roots. I wanted to point out that his overgrown beard and nasal hair put him outside any well-groomed woman's minimum standard, but it was clear he had his own minimum standards firmly in place.

The more I thought about it, the more it irritated me. How arrogant of men to have this minimum standard thing.

Until I realized all my girlfriends had been verbalizing their minimums since the second grade.

My first slumber party was an education in what was to come, everything from how to discretely buy tampons to the characteristics of the perfect boyfriend. I remember making a pact with my best friend Sarah in sixth grade that we would never, ever, hope to die, date a boy with too much hair on his arms. That was pretty easy until tenth grade when the guys grew some pretty serious body hair and we abandoned the pact.

So, I admit women have minimum standards too. But I didn't really want to know that men have them, because it forced me to accept the fact that I probably fall below the line for some guys. I know, it's obvious—every guy isn't dating me.

I finally came to grips with it when one of my guys friends said, "Minimum standards is just another way of saying 'chemistry.'"

"No it's not," I protested.

"Yes it is. It's just a way of saying, 'These things are what do it for me.' This is what I need in a woman to feel good about her and about myself."

"What do you mean by 'feel good about myself'?" I asked.

"I think a guy sets these levels more to feel good about himself. Probably starts in junior high when he feels really pathetic and decides two pathetic people can't have a good life together, so he better go after someone who's a little higher up the social ladder and can give him the ego boost he needs."

"That's pathetic," I said.

"Yep, it is," he agreed. "But remember, a guy in junior high and probably for a number of years after junior high, is a cross between a fantasy writer and a *Fear Factor* contestant. Even now I feel like I'm constantly trying to balance my dreams against my fears, especially with the women I date."

"So what does the minimum standard do for that?" I asked.

"Gives us a sense we have some control over the uncontrollable? Oh, I don't know," he responded in a voice reminiscent of defeat.

I changed the subject just to keep him from looking so miserable. We talked about football season and my car problems and finished talking before the conversation was really over.

I've decided there is a better way. We should all have stickers on our foreheads. Maybe like those labels they used to put on kid's clothes. People with elephant stickers are a good match with other elephants. If you have a giraffe on your forehead, don't even try to date an elephant or a moose or a duck. It won't work. Some online dating services try to do that with personality tests and interest inventories. I think the sticker idea is better.

But then again, you'd probably have some guy screw it all up by insisting that although he's a moose, his absolute minimum standard is a Siamese cat.

≪ ≫

10

"Guys like to be touched."

That was the gem I learned from Alex. Alex was this muscular hunk of a guy who worked out faithfully, ran three miles a day even in the rain, and never considered he might have a feminine side. He wasn't chauvinistic; he was all testosterone—raised in a family of four brothers with a very assertive, athletic mom.

Alex had no clue what the average woman thought or how she felt. He didn't need to. Women were willing to put up with his weaknesses in order to get their hands on his strengths, so he went through life believing he really connected with women. He thought he understood them well. He detested other men who purposely used women. And he liked to be touched. In his mind, that gave him a special connection to women.

"Everyone likes to be touched," I said to him during our intriguing discussion of personality and its effect on your choice of friends and lovers. "Don't you remember the studies about the babies in orphanages who died because they weren't touched enough?"

"Yes, but that's not what I mean," Alex replied. "I mean I would never consider dating a woman who isn't touchy enough."

"What?" I shot back.

"Any woman I date has to understand I need her to touch me the way only my woman can…and just for the record, I don't mean just in overtly sexual ways. I mean show tenderness and caring through her touch. Nurturing without mothering."

I looked at him across the table. I was a college senior facing graduation in a couple of months, and Alex was a second-year doctoral student who taught one of my upper division classes. He defined the successful, attractive man. Yet, here he was confiding in me after only a few weeks. He was showing vulnerability. I wondered why since I was dating someone else and clearly not available.

"Why do you think non-sexual touch is so important to you?" I asked.

"I don't know," he answered, looking away. "If I were a psych major, I'd probably say it was a lack of female siblings or an unfulfilled desire for my mother's nurturing, but I really don't think so."

"Maybe it's just your nature...your personality. Maybe under all those muscles is the heart of a softie," I suggested.

"Yeah, maybe, but more likely I have hypersensitive nerve endings which respond by producing endorphins when I'm touched." He looked directly at me then smiled a mischievous smile and waited for me to volley back.

I decided to avoid the easy comeback about hypersensitive nerve endings. We were just friends, and I wanted to keep it that way.

"Do you think all guys are like that?" I asked.

"I think there are more of us than women realize. We're not always about sex...well actually we are." He smiled. "But sometimes we're tired or stressed and we need to be touched and to feel connection. It's one way a woman shows me she cares, and I like it a lot."

After that conversation, I started noticing something interesting. Men were being touched all around me, in restaurants and theaters. Couples were holding hands everywhere. Connection was defusing stress all over town. I started to appreciate the value of even small touches. Not the premeditated and overly sincere touches that appear fake or the disgusting, invading touches of control or manipulation. The ones I came to appreciate were the ones that said, from one person to another, you matter and life just wouldn't be as good without you. It isn't only men who like to be touched that way.

≪≫

11

"Do you think it's normal for a guy to stay in his cave for weeks at a time?" Jen blurted out early one morning as soon as I picked up the phone.

"What do you mean?" I asked, rubbing my eyes and glancing at the clock. It said six forty, and I didn't have to be up until seven.

"Well, do you think it's a normal cycle in a marriage?"

"I'm no expert at marriage, but I guess it's not uncommon," I ventured. "Why are you asking before seven in the morning?"

"Because something doesn't feel right to me," Jen said. "And I can't put my finger on it."

"Well, maybe it would help to define the 'something' that doesn't feel right," I said, sitting up in bed and pulling the covers over my shoulders. It was cold, and the heater hadn't come on yet.

"Okay, I'll try," Jen said.

I rubbed my eyes and mentally noted that I only had about fifteen minutes to listen before my morning became a train wreck.

"Charlie has been working more hours in a time when construction has slowed. And he doesn't seem to want..." her voice trailed off for a moment, "to want to touch me as much as he used to."

"Oh," I said, my voice heavy. It didn't take much to put two and two together and come up with an affair. We both had to be thinking the same thing because the silence was thick and choked our words. Clearly, this was the first time Jenny had verbalized her concerns to anyone. I searched through every file drawer in my mind for something titled "How to Comfort Your Sister When Her Husband Is Having an Affair." Nothing came up.

"Jen, I don't know what to say," I finally stammered.

"Me either." She began to quietly sob. "I just can't believe this is happening to me, and I don't know what to do."

"Do you need me to come over?" I asked. There must be a section of my company's employee manual that allows bereavement days for this kind of grief. If not, there ought to be.

"No, I'm okay," she said. "Besides, I have to get the kids up and ready for school. I just needed to talk with you for a couple of minutes so I don't lose it in front of the kids. They're too young for this."

"You know I love you, and I'm here for you," I said as I slid out of bed.

"I know," she replied. "Love you too."

≪ ≫

12

Jen didn't bring up her marital concerns again for over a month. In fact, she avoided the subject and kept up a constant barrage of trivial details whenever we were together. We met for lunch and talked constantly about mutual friends, Thanksgiving plans, and her kids' school projects. It was clear to me she didn't want any break in the conversation that would allow doubt and fear to creep in.

I didn't see Jen and Charlie at all until Halloween. I was busy with work, friends, and studies. Besides, in my mind, looking directly at Charlie over and over would put a damper on my holiday cheer. I made it through trick-or-treat night with the kids by concentrating on the candy and the costumes. It was hard to smile directly at the guy who was cheating on my sister. The scum.

Our family planned to spend both Thanksgiving and Christmas Eve together. Jen and Charlie would be at his folks' for Christmas Day, so I was trying to figure out how to be civil to Charlie as we made holiday plans. I even allowed myself to secretly wonder once what his mistress would be doing while he was with us.

"Promise me you won't say anything or act differently toward Charlie during the holidays," Jen said to me when we met at the mall one afternoon. It was the first time she'd directly broached the subject since our phone conversation a month before.

"You mean you don't want me to confront him in front of the entire family just for fun," I said, trying to ease the conversation with a joke. Jen wasn't feeling the humor. She didn't reply.

"I'm sorry," I said. "I know this isn't funny, and you're really worried."

"Yeah, I am." She nodded.

"So do you want to talk about it?" I asked.

There really wasn't that much to talk about. Like a good sister, I fully engaged in the ten-minute conversation that revealed very little. Jen didn't know anything more than she'd known a month before. She just had a gut feeling something wasn't right, and it was hard to ignore the signs of an affair. The problem was, Charlie didn't actually seem like the affair type. Since he'd met Jen, he'd never shown any interest in other women.

She'd checked his computer, and he wasn't into porn or chat rooms. Yes, he had a superiority complex the size of Texas, and women were likely attracted to his combination of dress and success. Even I had to admit, he still looked pretty sharp for a middle-aged guy. But he didn't show signs of a midlife crisis. So why would he have an affair?

I left the mall that afternoon wondering what the future held for my sister. The sister who could in one afternoon redecorate a child's room, plan a major event for a client, cook dinner, and do it all looking like a runway model. No sweat. Neither of us was used to Jen's life being out of control. If it started spinning sideways, I feared it could change the balance of my universe too and have a cumulative effect on the entire region. Something dawned on me that day. My sister was my stability...my documented proof that hard work, good looks, and solid values paid off. If something bad happened to her and her family, my stability was going to take a big hit.

My anger at Charlie grew to a slow boil.

<< >>

13

My relationship with my dad is amazing. He's always had a way of making me want to please him, inspiring me to make him proud, assuring me there is nothing that could change his love for me. His love is constant, unconditional, pure. That's why the ersatz love I received from my first boyfriend was so insufferable.

We were nine and in the midst of daily fourth-grade traumas, so we attached ourselves to one another like barnacles in a storm. He carried my books and gave me bragging rights with my girlfriends in exchange for kisses, hand-holding, and full-frontal hugs. It was my first dating experience and I took it slow.

I don't remember when I realized his love wasn't like my dad's, but one day I knew it, and it felt like chewing used, tasteless gum. I looked at him one day and knew he was my boyfriend because we needed each other, not because he loved me unconditionally through time eternal. I clearly saw he was mine only until we broke up, at which time, I would probably see him walking the halls with another girl and have to swallow my pride about twenty times a day.

I wanted no part of this kind of love. I wanted perfect, unconditional, forever love or nothing.

That night, after everyone had gone to bed and my dad was watching the news alone in the family room, I snuck out of my bedroom and cuddled up next to him in his oversized recliner.

"Daddy," I asked tentatively, "will any boy love me the way you do?"

My dad left the TV on, but it was obvious I had all his attention. "What makes you ask that, honey?"

"I don't know…" I paused. "I just don't feel like anyone loves me like you do."

"That's because you only have one Daddy," he said gently as he stroked my hair. "I love you like only a daddy can." We both looked at the TV for a moment. A car was speeding down the freeway with law enforcement in pursuit. "And," he continued after a few seconds, "I love your mom as only a husband can."

That was a new thought to me. I knew my dad loved my mom. They argued sometimes, or as Dad liked to put it they discussed things loudly. But I was confident they loved each other. The idea that he loved her in a singular way—"as only a husband can"—that was a revelation to me. It made me feel slightly less special. I wondered why.

"So you love me and sis and mom…all differently?" I asked.

"Yes, I guess you could put it that way."

"Well, who do you love most?"

My dad paused. Years of living in a houseful of women had taught him well—he always answered these questions with care, slowly tiptoeing around the potential landmines. "The most?" he repeated slowly. We both watched TV for a moment as he gave the question more consideration. "Well, honey, what do you need most to live: water, light, or air?"

"Dad…don't answer my question with a question," I whined. "You always do that."

"I love each of you. Your mom is the woman I gave my heart to many years ago, and she feels like a part of me. You and your sister are my children, and I see myself in you and have loved you since the day I first knew you were going to be born. The three of you are like water, light, and air to me. I couldn't live without any of you."

I nestled close to him, laid my head on his chest, and fell asleep, secure and happy. I remember the strength of his arms as he carried me to my bed. Somehow the muscles in his arms and the security of unconditional love will always be intertwined in my mind.

Maybe that's why I can't imagine myself loving a man who's weak in either category.

≪ ≫

14

Dave's mother died a month before I met him. He sat next to me at the Wednesday morning meeting known as "a cure for insomnia"—a meeting so boring our team leader could put herself to sleep in mid-sentence. Dave and I started texting each other the third week. Fortunately for us, we rarely missed anything important.

Dave wasn't the kind of co-worker who talked much. He was pretty much all business with his expensive ties and well-researched comments. He could have been mistaken for a by-the-book attorney except at these particular meetings when he was bored and had a cell phone handy. Then he transformed into that guy in the back row of high school English class who had a quick wit and a bad attitude.

Most of the time Dave and I sent brazenly funny text messages about boredom or, when we felt particularly brave, about someone in the room. From time to time when I noticed Dave's eyes looking particularly sad, I'd ask how he was doing.

At first, he'd reply succinctly: "It's tough" or "I'm surviving." But about the sixth month after his mom's funeral, Dave replied, "Let's talk later." Three words instead of two—he was opening up.

We decided to meet for lunch at the deli with the great soup/sandwich combo and the private booths.

I wasn't sure how to begin a conversation about grief, but I didn't need to worry. Dave was ready to talk. This guy had been grieving alone in his cave for six months, and he was ready to venture into the more vulnerable "grief among friends." He took one bite of his turkey sandwich, looked directly at me, and said, "I never realized how much I'd miss my mom."

I gave him the "tell me more" look and said nothing. I was afraid one wrong word would make the man jump back in his shell like a hermit crab.

"It's not like I can't make it without her. I just really miss her." Dave glanced around the room as though he were looking for comfort in the pictures on the wall. With his big hazel eyes and slightly tousled brown hair, he looked like a sad little boy. We sat in silence for a minute or two as he ate slowly.

"It's okay to miss her," I said. "I know I'd miss my parents if something happened to either one of them."

"Yeah, you would," Dave said. "You'd miss the little things…the phone calls, someone who knows your favorite food and can remember when you were little. Those are the things you'd miss."

The noise in the deli faded as I began to think. My parents were the only people who really cherished my childhood. My aunts and uncles had known me as a child, but their memories were clips rather than the whole movie. When my parents die, the people who know my history best will be gone. I was jolted by the self-centeredness of that thought and by its harsh reality.

I looked over at Dave who was picking at his chowder. There was no way I could share my thoughts. They sounded too egotistical. Apparently Dave was thinking something he couldn't share either. We sat in silence for some time as people around us shared animated conversations. It was as though the entire world was going on with life and we were standing still.

Dave broke the silence. "You know," he said, with a combination of sadness and resignation. "Grief is very isolating."

I nodded.

"It's like you're in a boat all alone. Even though you can see other people and they may even row out to help you from time to time…you're still in the boat alone. No one else can do the work of grieving for you. You just have to keep rowing your own boat and hope you get closer to the shore."

He looked intently at his glass of tea then suddenly looked directly at me and commented as if he were relating a pertinent fact at a business meeting, "They say dying soldiers most often call for their mother. I guess we're all just little boys inside…boys who will always want our moms."

44

I reached across the table and put my hand on his arm. "It's got to be hard to lose a mom," I said.

Dave nodded.

"You know I'm here if you ever need to talk."

"I know," he said. But we both knew he wouldn't talk much.

He would grieve alone on long walks with his dog or in the privacy of his condo. I wasn't his wife or his girlfriend. I was a coworker, and neither of us wanted to blur the boundaries.

Dave taught me there are some things in life you must face alone. They aren't welcome or desired, but they're real and predictable.

That day in the deli, I realized someday it would be my turn to get personal with grieving. Someday it would be me seeking comfort and me single-handedly rowing my boat to shore.

≪ ≫

15

I have a no-tolerance system for my vehicle. I put gas in, change the oil regularly, and faithfully attend to the thirty-, sixty-, and ninety-thousand mile maintenance. In return, my car should never break down. Never. Period. One particular morning my car ignored its part of the agreement.

So there I sat on the side of the road, forty-five minutes late for work, waiting for AAA to come and figure out why there was a troubling amount of steam hissing out of the engine compartment. I don't remember which college boyfriend had taught me how to open my hood and determine whether the problem was water or smoke-based, but I remembered how to do it. I opened the hood of my car and saw white steam hissing out of a radiator hose. It's pretty hard to miss the radiator. Even I can find that.

The guy from AAA arrived, confirmed it was a radiator problem, and told me, "Don't feel bad. These things happen all the time now that they're making radiators out of plastic."

"What?" I asked incredulously. I'm no mechanical genius, but even I know if you heat and cool plastic a few hundred times, it's going to crack. Radiators aren't supposed to crack. They have an important job—hold water or the car overheats. My mind instantly determined there was a serious design flaw here.

"Yeah," the tow truck driver said. "Car manufacturers went to plastic radiators a few years ago to reduce weight and increase mileage, and so you end up replacing the radiator, the thermostat, and a few hoses about every five years now."

Great. That's what I needed. Regularly scheduled major repair on my basic transportation. That just wasn't what I envisioned for my expendable income when I headed to work every morning.

I'd like to say the day improved after my car was towed in and the mechanic assured me he'd have it done in two days. I'd like to say my attitude improved when my sister came to pick me up, take me to lunch, and deliver me to the rental car office. But the truth is, nothing improved. The sour feelings settled into my brain and refused to move. I was miserable and generously shared those feelings with colleagues, family, and friends. By the end of the day, no one wanted to be within fifty feet of me. So I drove home and felt sorry for myself in front of the TV.

The next morning I was still irritated and looking for more reasons to feel pathetic. After all, here I was stuck in life alone against my wishes while my sister, who for the record isn't nearly as gentle and kind as me and should, for that reason alone, have married at least five years after me, is married. She was the one with the SUV, the great kids, the house, the entire list of things I wanted. Yes, I acknowledged her husband might be a lying, miserable cheat, but the more I thought about it, the more I felt like an impoverished waif who would never escape the caste into which I was born and would have to spend my entire life begging for crumbs.

It's truly amazing how a car repair and a few hormones can send me into the underwater caverns of despondency where I sit until all the air in my tank runs out and I'm forced to the surface gasping for air.

I was sitting at my desk when Dave walked by. Dave and I were still texting each other during meetings and had bestowed upon ourselves the title of "Back Row Cool" within our company. We had a superiority complex that manifested itself through an aren't-we-amazing smile exchange when we met in the hallways. Today, Dave gave me his usual smile as he walked by, and when I didn't return it, he took three steps, stopped, and stuck his head back through my door.

"Hey, what's going on?" he said with a questioning look.

"Oh, nothing serious," I replied with a lack of enthusiasm that surprised even me. I like being around Dave, so I'd expected my voice to sound marginally happy. No such luck.

"It's just my car's in the shop, and I hate car trouble," I said.

"Oh, that sucks," he replied. "What happened?"

Fifteen minutes later, after he'd listened to my frustration with my car, automakers, plastic radiators, rental car companies, and life in general, Dave leaned over my desk.

"I know it's frustrating to dump money into car repairs. I hate that too. But sometimes when life is frustrating, you just have to focus on the positives in your life. You do have a lot of good going on, don't you?"

I had to admit some good things had happened in my life recently. I had just gotten a raise and was in negotiations with my landlord to purchase my condo. My sister and I were getting along really well, in spite of her current situation. I only had one year of master's classes to go and a promising job trajectory after graduation.

Dave saw the list cascading through my mind. He leaned even further over my desk, looked right into my upturned eyes, and said these words, which have been ricocheting around my mind ever since:

"Don't focus on one glass of spilled milk when you have a full gallon sitting in your refrigerator." I'm a chick, and I'll admit I didn't really want to hear that right then. I wasn't hormonally open to uplifting thoughts. I wanted sympathy in four variations.

Dave smiled at me the way men do when they feel they've solved a problem. Satisfied, he headed off to his office. I sat there a couple of minutes feeling like no one would ever understand how hard it was to be me, and then, miraculously, I started thinking about the gallons of milk in my refrigerator. The visual of that particular metaphor has never left me.

I started to realize that even in the hardest situations, you have to open the refrigerator door and look. Even Jen has some milk left: her kids, her job, our parents, and me. It made me feel strangely content to realize I was a good thing in Jen's difficult world. It also made me realize my car problems didn't truly compare to Jen's problems. It was a matter of perspective: Einstein's theory of relativity in an emotional realm.

Of course, I still get irritated when there's spilled milk in my world. It's messy and wastes my valuable time. But I've never forgotten Dave's words. When you compare the gallon in the fridge and a spilled glass, there's really no comparison.

≪ ≫

16

Thanksgiving went smoothly despite the fact that I could see Jen wasn't as affectionate toward Charlie as usual. My parents were too immersed in grandchildren to notice, and I kept my promise and didn't hint.

Right after Thanksgiving, Jen entered her "I can't take this" phase. She was tortured and torn between knowing the truth and avoiding the facts, so she focused on her children until her brain overflowed with emotion and her eyes blurred with tears.

"I don't know how much longer I can handle this," Jen sobbed one morning after she'd successfully kept it together and fed everyone breakfast. "My husband feels as distant as the North Pole, my kids are completely oblivious, and here I am in the middle, trying to hold this family together. It's torture. I just want to run away or scream or curl up in fetal position and sleep, but I can't. I have to keep pretending everything is fine because I can't prove it isn't.

"I think it—I feel it in my gut—but I can't prove it." She was beyond crying now. The words had so much emotion; I didn't know what to say. I knew Jen was terrified her marriage was going to crumble in her hands and kept hoping her silent love for Charlie would somehow bring him back. The problem was, she didn't know where he had gone—or if he'd taken someone else with him.

"Look, you have to focus on the kids and yourself right now," I said. It was all I had, whether it was good advice or not. "Just take care of them and keep your business afloat. No matter how things turn out, you're going to need healthy kids and your income."

"You're right," Jen said with little conviction. "I have to focus on something tangible or I'll go crazy worrying." I knew Jen could keep that focus for a while, but eventually her personality would demand resolution, even if that meant confronting Charlie's mistress face to face.

December arrived in California carrying sunglasses and a beach chair. It was unseasonably warm for the first few days, and after the cool overcast weather of Thanksgiving it was a dramatic change. The warmer weather seemed to supercharge Jen; she became a dedicated and detail-oriented sleuth. Instead of checking Charlie's computer periodically to see if he was surfing porn sites or emailing women, she began daily checks of everything: pants pockets, the stain on the sleeve of his shirt, credit card bills. The fact that she didn't find anything made the search even more imperative. Either Charlie was innocent or he was purposefully, deceitfully playing cat and mouse with her.

Charlie had a history of being arrogantly intelligent, wanting to prove his superiority in select situations. Was he actually capable of maliciously living a double life? The very thought infuriated both of us.

"I just don't know what's going on," Jen said pointedly when I picked up the phone at work one morning. "There's nothing. No receipts, no lipstick stains, no nothing. Either he's just bored with me and pulling away for no reason or he's the biggest lying cheating jerk on the planet."

"Yeah," I agreed. It was hard to openly respond to that last sentence from the professional atmosphere of my desk.

"I just don't know what to do," she said, her voice unsteady. "I can't take this. I have to confront him. But," she hesitated, "what do I say? I just don't know what to say. How do you accuse someone without any hard evidence?"

"Jen," I said gently. "Give yourself time to think. You'll figure out what to say. You're a wise woman."

"Yeah, but not wise enough to keep my husband," she said, her voice cracking with emotion.

In all the years I've known my sister, I'd never heard her more despondent. I was starting to worry, seriously worry about her. She'd never been an alarmist before. She was the assertive businesswoman whose instincts and acumen had proven themselves many times. She was the one I counted on to be logical and stable. Now she was falling apart in front of me, vacillating between anger and anguish.

I left work early and went directly to their house. The kids were playing with Legos and harassing each other. Jen was cooking in the most robotic way. I stayed all evening. Charlie called once to say he was working late, and he didn't come home until after I left. At least I assume Charlie came home. I never asked. My fear had become as palpable as Jen's. Something was seriously wrong.

≪ ≫

17

Jen decided she wasn't ready to confront Charlie. She needed some counseling first; things were too uncertain and she was afraid to cause irreparable damage with an outright accusation. She couldn't get past the fact there was no direct evidence of an affair; it was all circumstantial. In fact, truthfully, there wasn't even circumstantial evidence. It was basic woman's instinct. But still, her instinct was compelling.

Jen and Charlie had been attending a large local church since they were first married, so she called the church office, said she had a friend who was considering counseling, and got a few recommendations.

It truly surprised me when Jen told me she'd looked at the list of names and made her decision based on the sound of each counselor's name when she said it out loud. My sister has always been the paramount decision-maker who considers things logically and unemotionally. But here she was choosing a counselor by the sound of a name. I knew then for sure she'd become desperate for answers. Any answers at all.

She chose Dr. Lorrayne Neval. She said the name sounded comforting. Dr. Neval's office was in a group of Cape Cod-style office buildings. It was an unusual setting for coastal Southern California, but I had to admit when we drove by on the way to pick up groceries that next weekend, Dr. Neval's office looked like a place you could share your secrets. The only problem I had with Dr. Neval was the horrible tendency my mind had to turn her name into Dr. Navel. *Navel* wasn't nearly as comforting as *Neval*.

Jen's first appointment came and went with no great breakthrough. After all, you need at least one hi-how-are-you visit before you launch into my-husband-is-a-lousy-lying-cheat. Jen had too much pride and reserve to dump the entire truckload of accusations on the doctor's floor in the first hour, so she talked about her kids and the early years of marriage, only briefly touching on the subject of her deteriorating relationship with Charlie. After twenty minutes of historic perspective, Dr. Neval gently asked, "What brought you to my office during this busy holiday season?"

"I just didn't know what to say," Jen told me later that afternoon. "How do you say to someone you barely know, 'I have no proof, but I think my husband has replaced me, the bastard'?"

I didn't even try to answer. Jen was irreplaceable to me, so I puzzled over the concept that Charlie could have replaced her.

I know—I've heard the jokes about men trading their forty-year-old wife for two twenties. I've heard the horror stories in the nail salons about women who gave the best years of their lives to the bum. But somehow my mind just couldn't wrap that around Charlie. Somehow the stereotype didn't fit.

Maybe after nine years of being his sister-in-law, I didn't even know Charlie. We all know someone who lived next to a serial killer for fifteen years and thought he was a just a loner—a quiet, odd guy. Who knew he kept body parts in the fridge? Well, maybe I didn't personally know someone who lived close to a serial killer, but...

My mind can play with the oddest thoughts sometimes. Fortunately, Jen said something about wanting to get the most from her investment in counseling, and I had the presence of mind to agree, so our conversation seamlessly reconnected over the idea that $175 an hour is a lot to pay unless you plan to open up and get to the heart of the problem.

Somehow I thought Dr. Neval would appreciate hearing more than kid stories at the next appointment.

« »

18

Lots of people have a Christmas story. Most tell sweet tales full of inspirational value. I have a few of those in my repertoire, but the one with the thorny ending is more interesting. It was my sophomore year of college. I was in the process of dumping loser number two in a string of three, and I was stuck in the dorm until vacation surrounded by couples and pseudo-couples who were reeking true love. The scent of it made me miserable.

There is no good time to break up, but early December is especially cruel. I'd tried to make things easier by becoming seriously unavailable all the time and purposefully coughing regularly to make it appear I was on the verge of walking pneumonia. I mentioned how hard it was to devote time to any relationship just before finals and how it wasn't fair to him. He didn't take those hints and frustratingly became even more attentive. There was just no getting around the fact I had to tell him, directly and quickly.

It's times like this a girl lets down her parent-child defenses and turns to her dad for advice. My dad had always been a source of quality usable information. He was the one who explained why stars twinkle at night, why fire burns with different colors, and why three days a month my mother got freakishly upset over little things. His answers always made sense without overwhelming me. I needed that kind of an answer now.

Girlfriends would talk about protecting my boyfriend's feelings and finding the right place and what to wear on a break-up date. I'd already decided I was past protecting his feelings, there was no good location for a break-up, and I was going to wear my cheap jeans. I needed a bottom line answer from a male perspective.

It wasn't hard to find my dad when I was ready to talk. I can't tell you why, but whenever I call his cell phone, he always picks up. I know he has meetings and appointments, but he's nearly always accessible, and I love that about him. When I called this time, he picked up on the second ring.

"Hey, Dad."

"Hi, Cutes."

"Got a minute to answer a tough question?"

"Sure," he said. "Let me send this e-mail real quick and then I can talk."

I heard a click, a shuffle, and he was back.

"So what's up?" he asked, his full attention focused on my voice.

"I have to break up with this guy, it's nearly Christmas, and he doesn't seem to be picking up on my hints like being unavailable and uninterested. Got any advice?"

"Let me tell you something, sweetheart," Dad said. "Men don't take hints."

"Yeah, I noticed," I said.

"We men are basic creatures. You can't hint around with us. The only way to break up with a guy is to say, 'Look, it's over. Lose my number. Don't call me again. If you come within thirty feet of me, I'm going to get a restraining order.'"

I burst out laughing.

"No, baby, I'm not kidding," he said with a smirk in his voice. "You think I'm joking, but I'm telling you the truth. Men don't take hints."

"Oh, come on, Dad," I said, still smiling. "I can't be that mean. I'll probably say something like, 'Look, this isn't working out for me, so I think we should just be friends.'"

"You could say that if you wanted," Dad said. "But in his mind it will translate as 'Maybe there's still hope, so keep pursuing.'"

"How could he interpret 'keep pursuing' out of that?" I asked.

"Because it's not goodbye and lose my number," he answered. "It doesn't sound final. It sounds like a hint, and hints are interpreted by the receiver's desires not the sender's intentions."

I sighed so loudly it surprised me. They say sighing is a sign of sadness. "That's so brutal," I said. "I wouldn't want anyone to break up with me like that."

"That's because you're not a guy," Dad said. "I've had it both ways, and I really preferred the straightforward 'It's over. Don't call me anymore.' That way I didn't waste any more time on someone who had no interest. I didn't wonder if there was still a chance, and I moved on quickly."

"How could any woman ever break up with you, Dad?" I asked. "You're the best man in the world."

I could almost hear my dad smiling over the phone. "You're sweet, my darlin' daughter," he said. "Fortunately, quite a few women weren't interested, and it gave me the freedom to move on and find your mother, who just happens to be the best wife in the world."

"So you really think I should just blurt out, 'It's over, move on'?" I asked.

"Yes, I really do," he answered.

"Okay. I love you, Dad. Thanks for the advice."

When I hung up, I knew he was probably right. But I also knew I'd never find the man-killing instinct necessary to shoot someone down with my words just before Christmas.

So I gently told this poor guy we should go back to being friends, and it took him two more weeks to absorb the full impact. I went home for Christmas wishing I'd ripped off the band-aid rather than pulling it off one hair at a time. The next time I broke up with someone I simply said, "It's over. You should lose my number and move on."

It wasn't the easiest thing I've ever done, but it wasn't as hard as I'd expected.

≪≫

19

December snuck up on me this year like a pouncing tiger. I should have listened to my intuition, but like a foolish gazelle, I ignored the predator in the bushes. By the time I saw the inevitable coming it was too late. Christmas was twenty-nine days away and I'd done no shopping, and I mean none...as in absolute zero.

I suppose I could forgive myself. After all, my sister was in crisis, and an attentive man named Austin was distracting me.

When I first saw him, I thought he was too young for me. He had the face and build of a college student with short brown hair and deep-set blue eyes. He looked like someone who drove around in a Jeep Wrangler and wore board shorts all day, but actually he was a lot closer to my age, drove a Mercedes, and wore suits to work. His office was in a building around the corner from my office. Who would have guessed?

We met at a bakery one day when I was craving a bagel and he was grabbing coffee on his way to work. We chatted in line, exchanged business cards under the premise of expanding our professional contacts, and I walked out smiling. He called the next day.

Sometimes I wonder why people name their kids after cities. Austin, Brooklyn...did the names come first or did the cities? These harmless questions were just another way I allowed myself to think of him at odd times.

Three days after we met, we were eating lunch together at Jerome's Deli, and four days later, he took me to dinner at a Thai restaurant that is now one of my favorites. Best of all, in two dates I hadn't seen any fatal flaws. Admittedly, two dates may not be enough to know with certainty that a man is free of such character defects as picking his teeth after meals or maxing out his credit cards for boy toys, but my intuition said not to worry. It wasn't necessarily comforting to realize this was the same intuition that had failed me before.

December hadn't been easy on Jen. In spite of two counseling sessions, her emotions were like fragile ornaments on a lopsided tree. One small movement and something was going to fall and shatter.

Charlie was unusually quiet when I saw him, which wasn't often. He looked sad or guilty—I couldn't really tell. But it was obvious that something had changed in their marriage. I found myself constantly looking for that one clue, that one missing puzzle piece that would allow me to wake up with the perfect answer for my sister's dilemma. I kept waking up, but the answer didn't materialize. Somehow I knew it was going to burst out all over Christmas and after this holiday nothing was ever going to be the same. It was that intuition thing again.

≪ ≫

20

Austin called me on Saturday morning two weeks before Christmas on the spur of the moment and asked me to join him for a walk. We had a great time behind the leash of his black lab, Axle, who sniffed and trotted his way through the park. Then we cruised through a few neighborhoods where large Christmas trees were perfectly centered in large front windows. You have to love Southern California Christmas—over-ornamented trees grilling in the sunshine.

We ended our walk with fish tacos at Tia's. I've always lived by the mantra that Mexican food is only good when it's dripping down your face. That bit of personal insight made Austin laugh and opened a conversation into our likes and dislikes, interests and hobbies.

We talked for nearly an hour about hobbies. His were varied: snowboarding and skiing because he couldn't decide which he liked better so he did both; skeet shooting because his father had introduced him to the sport at age eight and he liked the challenge; snorkeling because he loved the ocean and still had dreams of getting his scuba license; and golf because most people who wear suits to work need to play golf. We had a few hobbies in common. I love the snow, probably because my hometown never had any, and I love the ocean because I spent most of my childhood summers at the beach. I was intrigued by the skeet shooting and made Austin promise he'd let me try sometime. I was undecided about the golf. Truthfully, I thought it looked boring, but that opinion came more from ignorance than experience. While Austin and I talked, Axle dutifully ate anything that hit the sidewalk. It was such a relaxing yet stimulating Saturday. The experience made me itchy for the next date.

"This was fun," Austin said as we sprinted up the steps to my condo. "I know it's a busy time of year, but I'd love to see you again before the holidays."

At times like these, I've always wished I could think quickly enough to respond with wit and charm, but all that came out was, "Sure that sounds great."

"I'll call you tomorrow." He smiled over his shoulder as Axle pulled him toward the street and the guaranteed jog home.

I have to admit, Austin's smile was great and his biceps looked amazing as he tugged against the leash. This guy was pretty close to a 9.5 on my scale of 10. I refused to say he was a 10 because that would be a set-up for disappointment. A 9.5 provided a margin of error, so I could honestly tell myself I didn't prematurely fall for a loser if he turned out to be one. It's very hard on the ego to keep making the same mistake—to keep believing the next guy is going to be worth all the trouble and all the investment just before the emotional guillotine falls and heads tumble into baskets.

Although I didn't want to admit it, the issues between Jen and Charlie had taken my normal defenses toward dating and turned them into full-blown cynicism. After all, if Jen's Mr. Perfect could turn out to be a bored, cheating, lying jerk, and if my sister with all her amazing traits and out-standing intelligence actually married said jerk, well, how in hell did I stand any chance of doing any better?

A younger sister rarely scores better than the older sister. I'm sure there's a statistic somewhere to support that.

≪ ≫

21

I nearly cut my finger off one night using a dull knife. I know that sounds ridiculous, but it's true. I promised a girlfriend I'd make my famous roasted beet salad for her Christmas party, and, believe me, it pays to roast the beets ahead of time. Roasting beets the night before a party is torture—you end up with stained fingers that scream, "I don't attend to details like waxing" to every male in the room. So I was in the kitchen one evening a few days before the party, hacking away with this pathetic excuse for a knife, when I slipped and blood gushed.

Living alone has its advantages, but doctoring yourself isn't one of them. Lucky for me, I don't get queasy when I see blood. After I got the bleeding under control, I took a good look and decided it might need stitches. It looked a little deeper than dermis, and if I looked too closely or for too long I thought I could see bone. So I wrapped up my finger, added an ice pack for good measure, and drove to the nearest walk-in emergency clinic. Fortunately it wasn't a Friday or Saturday night, so I didn't have to wait long.

I have to admit, I was a little surprised when the nurse practitioner turned out to be a middle-aged man named Don. He walked in the room, sat down, and very gently removed my homemade bandages.

"So how'd you fillet your hand?" he asked, looking directly at the wound as I answered.

"Cutting beets for a salad," I admitted.

"Dull knife?"

"Yeah."

Don shook his head slowly.

"Dull knives are vicious weapons. They seem so innocent until they strike," he said, trying to be serious, but there was enough playfulness in his words to make me laugh.

"Yeah," I repeated, not knowing what to say. I felt like a nine-fingered idiot.

"Looks like you'll be okay though," he said as he worked on my hand. "I don't think you need stitches. Just leave this dressing on for two days, keep it dry, and then make sure it's clean and covered during the day until it heals. Watch for signs of infection: redness, swelling, hot to the touch. Take something over the counter for pain if you need it."

I walked out, got in my car, and started to cry. It's times like this I need a broad shoulder to cry on. No woman should have to endure a wound by herself. I knew Austin was at his office Christmas party, and besides, I wasn't ready to reveal my uncoordinated side to him just yet.

I sniffled my way home and called a couple of girlfriends, who as luck would have it couldn't come to their phone right now so please leave a message. I left messages in my most pathetic voice, but that did nothing for me on the sympathy scale, so I defaulted to the lowest common denominator of sympathy, my parents. Dad answered the phone.

"Hi, Cutes."

"Hi, Dad." Sniffle, sniffle.

"What's wrong, honey?"

"I nearly cut off my finger and just got back from the emergency clinic. No stitches, but it wasn't much fun." Now I'll admit I should have let go of the verbal "nearly cut off my finger" a few hours before. I didn't purposefully exaggerate; it just came out that way.

Mom got on the line so she and Dad could both listen patiently to the entire story. When I finished telling every detail and they'd given the requisite amount of parental sympathy, Dad spoke gently.

"You know, sweetie, maybe you should spend a few dollars and get some good knives."

I didn't think much more about that statement until a few weeks later when I heard a group of guys talking at work. They were talking about screwdrivers and Allen wrenches. They went into vivid detail about the merits of one brand over another and the necessity of buying an entire set of wrenches for every possible thirty-second of an inch. That's when it hit me.

Have you ever walked through the tool section of Sears? There are fourteen different kinds of hammers, about a hundred types of wrenches, and more screwdrivers and screws than clouds in the sky. You'd never catch men using a reciprocating saw when the project called for a circular saw. They aren't afraid to include the cost of tools in the overall cost of a project. Why was I?

That day something clicked. I decided it was time to invest in some tools around the house. The next paycheck, I took my clothing budget and bought three nice knives, one quality hammer, a cool screwdriver with eight interchangeable heads, and a dremel.

All right, I admit the dremel was an impulse buy. It just looked so handy. If I've learned anything from listening to men, it's this: you have to start buying quality tools even if you haven't fully decided on the project yet. After all, you never know what challenge you'll face next and you'd better be prepared.

≪ ≫

22

Austin and I had a wonderful third date, unless you count the fish taco morning as our third date. In that case, we had a wonderful fourth date. He took me to a new restaurant on the west side of town that required you know someone to get a Saturday night reservation, especially a Saturday night in December. I found out in the middle of my salad that his sister was the owner's girlfriend. Not just any girlfriend—she was an accomplished pastry chef at a hotel across town. So now I found myself surrounded by over-achievers. As if my sister didn't set the bar high enough.

I decided it wasn't smart to drive my mind down this particular rutted path, so I started playing the "I'm younger and prettier than she is" game with all the other women in the restaurant. They never know we're playing unless we make eye contact. Austin did a good job distracting me from the game before I realized I wasn't the prettiest woman in the room. Somewhere mid-entree he reached across the table and got my attention.

"I know I should have asked you before now," he hesitated slightly, "but if you don't already have plans for New Year's Eve, I'd love it if you would go with me to a party at my sister's hotel." His eyes didn't leave mine. I loved the amazing combination of vulnerability and anticipation on his face. It was tempting to make it last a little longer than necessary, but I was so excited to have a New Year's Eve date for the first time in two years I couldn't hold back my answer.

"That sounds like a lot of fun." I smiled and tilted my head slightly to appear extra-feminine. "I'd love to go with you."

By the way, I don't do extra-feminine well, so, not surprisingly, as I reached for my water glass I overshot and nearly knocked over both the glass and the candle.

It broke the spell, but it also broke the tension. The rest of the evening was a wonderful combination of laughter, interesting stories, and the right amount of flirting to make the thought of New Year's Eve even more enticing.

The delicious end of our third date sealed the deal. The kisses were sweet. The smell of Austin's skin and the touch of his hands made my body tingle. I couldn't wait for New Year's Eve. Now I just had to make it through Christmas Eve with Charlie on the other side of the table. The lying, cheating SOB.

《 》

23

I don't know if there's ever a good time to introduce a boyfriend to your family. No matter how well you plan it, there's always the pressure of "now things are getting serious." So frankly I was hesitant to drag Austin home to meet Mom and Dad. With the added complication of Jen's situation, I was actually avoiding it.

Austin and I had discussed our families. I knew quite a bit about his, and he knew the basics about mine. That's all I wanted to share. My normally normal family was problematic at the moment, and I didn't quite know how to verbalize any of that situation to him. Although I wasn't sharing a lot with Austin, my family was hearing his name fairly regularly.

Have you noticed in the early stages of a relationship, especially when you think there's a chance this might be a good guy and your parents and sister might actually approve, you just can't help yourself—you talk too much? Well, I started to toss Austin's name around in conversations, and my mother, ever the curious type, wanted to know more. I hedged a little. She asked a little.

We played conversational tetherball until she finally said, "So, honey, would you like to invite Austin to join us for Christmas Eve?"

I love that about my mother. Everyone's welcome. I've had Christmas invitations extended to roommates, friends, bosses, coworkers, and exercise class instructors. My mother believes no one should be alone during the holidays, and if she had the room she'd probably publish an open invitation on the Internet.

"Thanks, Mom," I said. "I think he'll be with his family this year. But maybe we could get together another time."

I knew Austin had already made plans to drive to Fresno for Christmas to spend three or four days with his mother, step-dad, and his two sisters' families.

Austin's father had died when he and his two sisters were young, so he had a very soft spot for the women in his life. At age twelve he considered himself the man of the house, and to prove it he kept a baseball bat under his bed and spare batteries beside his flashlight in the nightstand drawer. He was prepared to defend his home to the death if necessary. Of course I smiled when he told me that story.

When Austin was fourteen, his mother remarried, which could have been a head-butting ram's fight between Austin and his step-dad but had actually worked out well. Both Austin's mother and step-dad recognized the pitfalls of two unrelated males in one house and avoided them. Now he was on very good terms with his family and actually looked forward to holidays with his niece and two nephews.

"Christmas is always more fun when there are kids around," Austin told me. "I love their excitement and curiosity."

I had to agree. I loved watching Blake and Sophie open their gifts and play with new toys. It added sparkle to Christmas, beyond what eggnog could provide.

I broached the subject of parental visitation with Austin the next time we talked.

"Hey, my mother invited you for Christmas Eve," I told him. "But I know you're headed up to be with your family. So would you like to drop by my parents' house sometime this week to appease my mother's curiosity?"

"Have you been talking about me that much?" Austin asked with clear amusement.

"Let's just say your name has come up in a few conversations—mostly positive."

"Nice to know," Austin said. "Sure, let's drop by and I'll give it my best shot at a good first impression."

A couple of nights later, on our way to the mall to begin my horribly delayed Christmas shopping, we drove by my parents' house. Of course I'd called ahead to let them know. Now that they were empty-nesters, my parents had a curious habit of wearing fewer clothes around the house, and, well, it would just be too risky to drop in on them.

As we made the last turn and stopped in front of my parents' house, I reached for Austin's hand and squeezed it.

"You nervous?" I asked.

"Not really," he said. "Should I be?"

"No. It's all good." I smiled across at him.

I know the story would be much more romantic if my parents lived in a quaint little neighborhood with tall trees lining the street and peonies in the garden. They don't. My parents live in one of those southern California neighborhoods built in the 1970s by a large developer. Their house is one of over 500 based on four floor plans. If you look carefully, their house looks exactly like the Harrington, Jackson, Chavez, and Peterson homes, which you can easily see from our front yard. These tract homes had been the staple of the Southern California middle class when my parents bought theirs in 1979.

If you looked at my parents' home from the outside, you'd see nothing special, except maybe the little grouping of five birch trees in the front yard. Although birch trees became popular in later years, very few of our neighbors had the interest or foresight to plant those in the seventies. The trees are a visual reminder to me that my parents' house is unique and special. Very special. Not because of the architecture or the furnishings or the plum location—because it's a home that's built on respect and love.

From the moment you step in my parents' door, you feel welcome. Yes, I know, I'm their daughter and I'm supposed to say that. But it's true. I didn't have any doubt my parents would make Austin feel welcome. They'd done that hundreds of times before with all the visitors who had walked through their door and become friends of the family. I wasn't concerned about Austin feeling welcomed; I was more concerned about Mom and Dad's impression of him.

Dad had definite opinions about the quality of man his daughters deserved, and I knew Charlie had barely made the cut. And when Dad didn't think a guy was good enough, he had very skillful and subtle ways of letting the guy know. Dad was never unkind, but he could weed out the inferior stock as skillfully as a rancher protecting the quality of his herd. Sometimes I wondered what Dad said to guys when they were alone. Whatever it was, it was effective.

Mom answered the door and greeted Austin warmly. She brought both of us into the kitchen and offered us fresh cookies.

Something funny happens when your boyfriend meets your mother. You can almost see the analysis going on in his brain. It usually boils down to either *oh man, I sure hope she doesn't end up looking like that* or *whew, if she ages like her mother, life will be good.* Fortunately for me it's consistently been the latter. My mother looks great for fifty-plus. Believe me, I'm counting on those genes, and I'll be really frustrated if I don't get them.

Austin seemed to feel very comfortable in Mom's kitchen. Knowing he had a good relationship with his mom and sisters helped calm me, but I still couldn't relax completely until he had Dad's seal of approval. And by the way, where was my dad?

"Your dad's finishing a phone call," Mom said. "He'll be down in a minute."

"Anything important?" I asked.

"He's talking to your Aunt Dottie," Mom said. "We may have to make a trip back to Boston soon. Dottie is feeling a little overwhelmed with all the repairs her house needs, and since she's alone now, your dad thinks we should spend a week helping her this winter."

"That would be nice," I said.

Austin nodded.

Mom grabbed her oven mitt and took out the last batch of cookies.

"So how long have you lived in this neighborhood?" Austin asked.

"We moved here when the girls were little," Mom replied. "At the time, I didn't think we'd stay this long, but here we are in the same house with grandchildren now!"

"My mom says the same thing," Austin laughed. "She and my step-dad have lived in the same house in Fresno since I was twelve."

We all heard the sound of footsteps and turned to see Dad in the doorway. He smiled and extended his hand to Austin who stepped forward and shook it with confidence. It hit me how different it was to bring home a high school boyfriend versus an adult boyfriend. My dad used to intimidate the teenage guys just by walking in the room. You could almost see the sweat dripping off their palms as they tentatively shook Dad's hand. Now that I think back on those introductions, I distinctly remember my dad smiling as he gripped those poor boys' hands and shook them a little too hard.

"It's a pleasure to meet you," Austin said, the muscles in his forearm strong against Dad's grip.

"Glad you could come by," Dad said. "Sorry I was on the phone when you arrived."

"No problem," Austin said. "It gave us a chance to eat cookies in the kitchen, and they taste great." Mom smiled and glanced at me. Austin had won her over already.

"Do you have to rush off or do you have a minute to see my pride and joy in the garage?" Dad asked Austin.

That was a good sign. Dad didn't show his '55 T'bird to just anyone. After all, you had to be worthy of the time it took to shimmy around the boxes in the garage and remove the cover. Within seconds both men had vanished out the back door, leaving Mom and me alone.

"He seems like a very nice guy," Mom said instantly.

"I think he is," I said. "It's too early to tell where this is going, but so far it's good."

"Oh, you can tell pretty early on," Mom said. "I could always tell by the first or second date if a guy was going to treat me well or if he was more impressed with his own good looks and talent."

"Wow, you had skills," I said. "It always takes me months to tell if someone has fatal flaws."

Mom laughed. "Well honey," she said. "It's easy for me to appear astute now that I'm out of the game and I chose well. I only hope you find someone as wonderful as your father."

"That's what I'm looking for," I said. "Dad set the bar high, and I'm not willing to settle for anything less."

I've thought about that many times. When you're blessed with a great dad, when you're the apple of his eye or his little princess or any of the thousand terms there are for a great dad/daughter relationship, it does set the bar pretty high. And that seems to do one of two things. Either you believe all men are that good, lose your innate sense of cynicism, and tie yourself to someone who couldn't reach the bar with stilts or you refuse to settle for less than the best, spend a lot of time waiting, and hopefully get someone who can stand toe to toe, head to head with your dad.

I truly wanted to hold out for the second option, and I was curious to see if Dad thought Austin might be the guy. Mom and I talked for a while before the men came back into the kitchen. Both were smiling, which I took as another good sign of the evening.

"Well, clearly you have a guy with great taste," Dad said. "He likes you and he likes my car."

"I do—on both counts," Austin said.

Within a few minutes, we'd said our goodbyes and were headed to the mall. It was an easy exit—Mom had been hearing me complain about my to-do list for two weeks, so she was sympathetic and sent us off with hugs and cookies.

Two hours later, when I'd done about all the Christmas shopping I could stand and had half my list complete, Austin and I were still talking about families and Christmas gifts and meeting my parents.

"They seem like really nice people," Austin told me. "I can see why you're so secure and confident."

It took me a second to realize he'd just paid both me and my parents a very nice compliment. The more I thought about it, the more I liked his choice of words. To be called secure and confident as a twenty-eight-year-old single woman felt incredibly good. To realize I agreed with him felt even better.

I was secure in my family's love—secure enough to refuse a poor substitute from the men I dated. I knew my family valued and respected me. I expected that and more from a boyfriend and from a husband. And yes, I was confident—confident that I was a good catch and had some wonderful qualities to bring to a relationship. Confident that someday I would be the right woman for an amazing man.

Now I just had to see if that amazing man was going to be Austin.

≪ ≫

24

Have you ever noticed how men don't seem to get bored? Give a guy four hours and a roll of tin foil and he'll make a suspension bridge that can support two SUVs. Give two guys a ball and bungee cord and they'll invent a competitive game in no time. This part of testosterone never ceases to amaze me.

That's why, as I watched Charlie during Christmas, things made less and less sense. Charlie didn't act like a man who was itching to get out of my parents' house and rendezvous with his mistress. He didn't act like the men I'd seen driving new sports cars and flirting with their latest bimbo. He acted like a man who wasn't itching to do anything. He acted bored and lethargic.

My sister and I were in the kitchen helping Mom with the last-minute cooking. Dad and the kids were in the den watching one of the million showings of *A Christmas Story* strategically scheduled to coincide with meal prep. I didn't even notice Charlie wasn't sitting beside the kids until I went into the dining room to get a serving bowl. Charlie was sitting there like a child banished to his room just staring out of the window. If it had been my sister sitting there, I'd know right away—she needs a hug and a tissue. But I was completely taken back by seeing a man sitting there, apparently bored. He looked sad and small. Charlie is not a small man. Something was different.

I walked back into the kitchen. It was clear Charlie hadn't seen me, or if he had he didn't acknowledge my presence.

"Hey, Jen. Come look," I said quietly. I motioned toward the dining room. She followed silently.

We both looked at Charlie's back for a few seconds and then looked at each other with puzzled looks. Charlie loved *A Christmas Story*. He'd normally be right in there with my dad and the kids laughing at the hideous lamp and cheering the demise of the bullies. It wasn't at all like Charlie to sit alone. Was he watching for someone? Was he planning something?

Jen motioned me back to the kitchen. "If he wants to sit out there and be antisocial, let him," she said. "I'm getting used to it at home. It's like he just doesn't care anymore." Her voice had a terrifying resignation. "Whoever she is, she's completely changed him, that's for sure."

I thought about her words as I put olives in a crystal dish and coaxed napkins into their rings. Charlie was different, that was obvious. And in many ways, Jen was different too. Both changes were equally unnerving.

Charlie seemed to perk up during dinner. He and my dad spent time dissecting the football season until Mom got bored of that and changed the subject. Jen sat across the table from Charlie for the first time ever. She placed the kids on either side of her and then acted as if, surprisingly, there just wasn't any room for him. If my parents noticed, they didn't say anything. Maybe they thought she was being a thoughtful parent. I thought she was being defiant. It was as if my sister was saying, "You can't make me play this game anymore."

The presents this year were nondescript. The kids got exactly what they requested. I got a lovely necklace from my parents, which made me smile but also made me wish I was getting a necklace from someone other than my parents. Austin and I weren't quite to the jewelry stage yet. Jenny gave me a sweater and didn't sign Charlie's name to the tag. Everyone went home with an armful of gifts, and I went home with low-grade sadness. Something wasn't right, and to face it at Christmas was like getting coal in my stocking.

《 》

25

Jen's suspicions and Charlie's behavior were putting a rather heavy blanket over my holiday season, and frankly I missed the holiday cheer. So right after Christmas I started focusing on New Year's Eve. I figured it could be the one holiday that saved this year's season. New Year's Eve is an annual prom for grown-ups. In spite of my already stretched December budget, I gave myself permission to buy a new dress, got a bling pedicure, and prepared to dance until my shoes stopped me.

Things were heating up with Austin, and that only added to the excitement. He was back from Fresno after a food-filled Christmas with his family and now all his attention was being lavished on me. During the week between Christmas and New Year's Eve, we walked Axle one evening and made dinner at my house the next. We nearly got arthritic thumbs with all our texting. We were at that wonderful stage of attraction where two people become magnets, moving closer and closer toward an inseparable bond.

Things seemed to be getting better at Jen's house too. For some reason, two days after Christmas Charlie began acting more like himself again, talking with Jen about the kids and suggesting a summer vacation in Colorado. Whether something had changed inside Charlie or whether the affair had begun flaming out on its own, none of us knew. I only knew Jen's phone version which defied logic and explanation—Charlie had just reengaged. It was bizarre.

"Can you believe he's talking about a family vacation?" Jen asked incredulously after she'd filled me in on the change. She seemed shocked but also slightly encouraged.

"That does seem bizarre," I said.

"Then last night, he walked into the kitchen, wrapped his arms around me while I was rinsing dishes, and whispered, 'I love you,' in my ear. It was so unexpected." She paused for a moment, deep in thought. "I was too surprised to push him away."

"Wow." It was all I could think to say.

"Weird, isn't it?" Jen asked. "No explanation, no nothing. Just a hug and a whisper."

"Yeah, it is kind of weird. Maybe it's a step in the right direction," I offered.

"Maybe," Jen replied.

It didn't make any sense to me. But I wasn't going to take Jen's morsel of hope and bury it in an avalanche of complex questions, so I stuck to positive sound bites.

Honestly I didn't think of Jen and Charlie much that week. My mind was too busy thinking about Austin. Call me a hopeless romantic—I just knew good things were going to happen this New Year's Eve.

Austin picked me up at six. We were eating dinner at a fabulous restaurant overlooking the city lights at seven. By eight thirty we were nibbling pastries in the ballroom of his sister's hotel. I was so impressed by the array of pastries; I wanted to try them all. Then I remembered my dress didn't have much spandex, so I limited myself to a bite-sized lemon tart, a chocolate almond cookie, and caramel apple thing. I'm sure Austin's sister would die if she heard me describe her beautiful creation as a "thing." It deserved better, but I'm minimally educated in the fine art of pastries. It was the best I could do.

We connected briefly with Austin's sister and her boyfriend. She gave me a quick tour of her office and the kitchen. Then Austin and I danced our way through the night. We'd stop periodically and find a place to sit and have a drink, but mostly we danced. Just before midnight the band played "Love Me Tender," and Austin pulled me close to him in a slow dance. He was good. Not too good, which would have made me feel self-conscious and out-classed, but good enough to lead well and keep me from bumping into the couples who were determined to take up more than their share of the floor. I leaned into his body as we slow-danced and waited for the sounds of midnight.

The shouts and horns started from outside the room and built like a wave around us. Within seconds, people were kissing and blowing through paper horns the hotel had provided. Some were attempting to sing "Auld Lang Syne" in the same key as the band. It was bedlam, and I loved it. Austin and I were smiling and kissing. His kisses were full of warmth and anticipation; his arms felt strong around me. I felt like the most desired woman in the world as we walked out of the hotel and headed to my condo.

New Year's Eve meshed seamlessly and magically into New Year's Day. The sun rose long before we did. For the first couple of hours, we sat drinking coffee and flipping between the Rose Parade and cable channels. Then I made guacamole and dug out some carrots, and we nibbled our way through the football games. Frankly, my feet were a little sore. I'd sacrificed my feet for sexy New Year's Eve shoes. Spending the day barefoot cuddling on the couch was the perfect antidote.

Around noon, we brought Axle over and tried to encourage him to lie quietly on the rug. Technically I wasn't supposed to have pets in the building, so we snuck him up by the back stairs and I mentally prepared a statement in case someone saw or heard anything. This was Austin's and my first illicit act, and we played it out like two spies in a movie, looking around corners and using hand signals. It made us both laugh.

Late in the afternoon Austin kissed me goodbye and snuck Axle back into his car. I realized it was becoming harder and harder to watch him leave. If the last twenty-four hours were any indication, I was going to be seeing a lot more of Austin and this was going to be a very good year.

≪≫

26

My phone rang just after four a.m. At first I was floating too far away to hear, but the insistence and harshness finally woke me and I reached across my bed.

Jen's voice jolted me into reality.

Every family has the defining moment, that moment when time stands still and from that day forward, everything is referenced as "before" or "after." Maybe it's the moment a police car pulls up in front of the house and an officer knocks on the door with bad news. Or maybe it's the day the baby doesn't wake up or the drunk driver careens across the highway.

For our family it was the wee hours of January second when Jen called, her words spilling out, filled with emotion. She could barely talk she was shaking so badly. She wasn't exactly crying. She was too high on adrenaline to produce tears. I knew from her first word that the news was bad.

Jen had rolled over in bed at about three fifteen, realized Charlie wasn't there, and for some unknown reason, she knew she should get up and find him. Maybe he was sending an e-mail or making a call. Maybe she could finally catch him cheating on her and end the frustrating games. Maybe she'd finally discover the identity of her competition. So she slipped downstairs quietly, and when she didn't find Charlie by the phones or the computer, she went to see if his car was in the garage.

Instead of a missing car she found Charlie. He was slumped in a corner, head in his hands and a gun in his lap, rocking back and forth and crying. Jen knew she'd stumbled onto the scene of a suicide, only this time the victim was still alive.

"I felt this horrible wave of nausea," Jen said, her voice shaking and her words accompanied by small gasps. "I just slumped against the wall and... Charlie looked up.

"He looked up at me," Jen continued, "and moaned, 'I couldn't do it. I'm such a coward. I just couldn't do it.' Do you realize he was going to kill himself? He was going to..."

"Is he okay now?" I blurted out, fully awake now. "Are you okay? Is he all right? Do you want me to come over?"

"He's okay. He's alive," Jen said.

"Do you want me to come over?" I repeated.

Jen sighed heavily. "I don't know," she said. "It's late...I need to go to bed. I don't know."

She stopped, and I could hear her breathing heavily, trying to calm herself. My mind was just starting to comprehend the magnitude of her words, of the situation. I sat up in bed and turned on my lamp. The room suddenly felt very cold.

"I'll come right now if you want me to," I said.

"I know," Jen said. Her voice was barely a whisper. I could tell she had no ability to make a decision. Decisions took energy and she had none. It took me a minute to realize she'd stopped her story in the middle of finding Charlie.

"So what did you do after you found him in the garage?" I asked quickly.

"I walked over," she said, her voice shaking again punctuated with sighs and tiny moans I'd never heard before. "I just started talking softly to him. I told him, 'It's okay, honey. You must be very tired, why don't we just go up to bed.'"

I could picture my sister, grace under pressure, the calm in the storm, somehow finding the strength to hold it together. But I had no idea how.

"We walked upstairs," Jen said, "and...and I put him to bed." Her voice stopped suddenly, abruptly.

I felt my hands shaking as Jen began crying, trying to talk her way through the rest of the story.

"I tried to stay calm and just lay there and held him until he fell asleep," she said through her tears.

As soon as she felt his body twitch and knew he was asleep, she quietly left the room, went to the garage, hid the gun in a locked container, and fell apart. She called me thirty minutes later when she could finally catch her breath.

I had no idea what to say as she finished talking. Is there a manual somewhere that tells a sister what to do in these kinds of situations? Let me tell you, I'd pay good money for a manual like that because I was totally and utterly speechless, and my sister needed some reassuring words.

"I just don't know what to say," I finally mumbled.

"I know...I know," Jen said, the smallest amount of stability beginning to return to her voice. "Should I call nine one one or just call a doctor in the morning?"

"Now that he's asleep, what do you think nine one one could do besides wake him up and make a lot of noise in the neighborhood?" I asked.

"Probably nothing," Jen said. "I guess they'd take him to a hospital and put him on suicide watch for a couple of days, right? He'd be in...in a psych ward."

"Probably," I said. My mind was still spinning in a thousand directions, wondering what piece of the puzzle we were missing, what the jury would say at our trial if we made the wrong decision and he died.

"Do you think he took any pills or anything?" I asked Jen.

"Oh damn, I didn't think of that," she said rapidly. "Let me go check on him and see if there are any empty bottles in the medicine cabinet. I'll call you back."

"You want me to come over?" I offered again.

"No, I'm okay. I'll call you back in a minute."

Five minutes later Jen called back.

"Nothing is missing, and there aren't any empty bottles lying around. I've checked everywhere but under the furniture." Jen started to cry. "I just can't believe this. This can't be happening. It can't be real..."

I listened silently.

"I don't believe I just found my husband trying to kill himself."

"I know, Jen."

"I thought he was having an affair. I thought he was distant because he was cheating on me. I thought he was being a jerk. I never though he was suicidal."

"I know."

She talked between sobs. I listened quietly for another ten minutes then she went to check on Charlie, to be sure he was still breathing and sleeping. Jen called me six more times before dawn. Neither of us could sleep, and we could never firmly decide if I should go to her house or not, so we just stayed intravenously connected by phone. Between her calls, I lay in bed wondering how life could change so abruptly and so horribly in the matter of minutes.

It is like that though. We all know it. You go for a jog and get hit by a drunk driver. You reach for the dropped spoon and forget the garbage disposal is running. You go for a check-up and leave with a diagnosis. And in that moment, life is forever changed.

My sister's life would never be quite the same. Whatever she had believed about safety and security in her own home, in her own family, was forever gone. What would the future look like now? I had no clue, but I was pretty sure Jen was in for a terrifying ride.

≪ ≫

27

Whether or not it was the right decision, Jen chose to leave a voicemail for Dr. Neval at nine that morning while Charlie continued sleeping. Dr. Neval called her back almost immediately. It was a brief conversation that boiled down to one directive. Charlie needed to see a doctor and he needed care sooner rather than later.

Jen called the Family Medical Associates emergency line, and Dr. Baker agreed to see Charlie within the hour. Dr. Baker had been our family doctor since Jen was in elementary school. He had taken in associates one by one until now he was part of a thriving group practice near the community hospital, partnered with younger physicians who gave him the respect he deserved. Jen trusted both his experience and his recommendations.

Dr. Baker did a thorough assessment of Charlie's physical health and ordered blood work for a variety of depression-inducing illnesses. Then he sent Charlie to see a psychiatrist. Jen called me from the atrium just outside the psychiatrist's office while Charlie waited in the reception area behind a closed door.

"I don't know if they're going to hospitalize Charlie or not," Jen said, her voice sounding tired and stressed. "In some ways I just want to take him home and let him rest. In other ways, I want professionals taking care of him in case he tries anything again."

"I thought they always put someone under suicide watch in a locked facility for a couple of days," I said. That's all I'd ever heard from talk shows and novels.

"They usually do," Jen said. "But sometimes, according to Dr. Baker, they determine the person isn't a threat to themselves or others and send them home under closely monitored outpatient care. That's why we're here. To see what this doctor recommends."

"Oh," I said. "So when will you know?"

"As soon as the psychiatrist sees him," Jen replied. "I gotta go. They're going to call him in soon. Love you."

It turned out Charlie wasn't considered an immediate threat to himself or others, so after an hour of psychiatric evaluation, he signed a contract with the doctor and let Jen drive him home. The contract was interesting. In it Charlie promised he wouldn't attempt suicide, he would call the doctor's office and check in daily, he would openly share any thoughts of self-harm, and he would meet all his scheduled appointments. I wondered if a contract like that had any real effect on a post-suicidal person, but apparently it had an effect on Charlie. Jen told me later he'd wiped away tears with the back of his hand as he signed it.

The doctor told Jen she could call anytime and gave her his cell number. If she felt there was any threat, she could request involuntary admission. It was just one more rock Jen had to carry, but she nodded, made the appointments for the next two days, and they left. As soon as they walked in the house, Charlie went upstairs to sleep.

I was waiting in the kitchen when they returned. Jen had asked me to meet her there after I picked up the kids and walked them over to play with the Townsend twins.

"I'll be right back," Jen said, walking through the kitchen on her way upstairs to help Charlie settle in.

When Jen returned we began the process of baby-proofing the house for a grown man. Jen drove the gun and all the ammo over to Dad and Mom's house. Jen had called them as soon as the sun came up, so they were prepared but shaken. She would have gotten rid of the gun except it had once belonged to Charlie's grandfather, a World War II veteran who had left his grandson only two possessions: his gun and his watch. Giving either away without Charlie's consent would be unthinkable. So Dad and Mom put the empty gun in a locked cabinet and hid the bullets two rooms away. Jen stayed at their house for a while—talking, crying, and hugging. I took all the medications with overdose potential to my house. I thought briefly about the kitchen knives then realized suddenly there was no way to remove every lethal weapon from the access of a determined person. Fortunately, Charlie didn't seem determined. He seemed exhausted.

For the next four days I called in sick and stayed around Jen's house, helping her when she felt too weak to function, picking up the kids from school and dropping them off for an afternoon at Grandma and Papa's house. It was easier to let the kids spend the afternoon playing video games and getting grandparents' help with their homework than it was to explain why Daddy wasn't at work.

Charlie slept almost round the clock. He'd briefly appear, Jen would ask how he was feeling, he'd watch a little TV, and then he was asleep again. It felt predictable, but we couldn't be sure, so Jen and I were as alert as guards in a watchtower, constantly scanning for an odd behavior or unexpected movement.

At night, I slept with the guest room door open, listening for unfamiliar noises. Jen didn't sleep. Whenever Charlie moved in bed, she woke with a start. She couldn't relax until she heard the sound of shallow breathing and felt Charlie's body twitch. Then she'd lie awake thinking, wondering, questioning for hours until sleep finally came in short and ineffective bursts.

I hadn't expected this level of insecurity or sleep deprivation from Jen, but it appeared almost immediately and slowly started eating away at her insides. She was exhausted, yet she remained alert while Charlie slept.

At night, I'd lay awake listening for Jen. When she left her bedroom, I would tiptoe to the kitchen and sit with her, our hands wrapped around steaming cups of tea. We would talk or we would sit together in silence, waiting for the fog of sleep to roll in. It was as unpredictable as weather. We thought about asking Dr. Baker for sleeping pills, but sentries can't do drugs. So we stayed awake and alert.

Sometimes when the house was quiet and everyone else was in their room, I would doze or read or think. I kept trying to figure things out. Puzzle pieces seemed to be lying on the floor at my feet, but I didn't have the strength to reach down and put them together. Jen needed too much support right now. I was using all my energy and strength to support her and her family, which left me completely exhausted. The problem was, I couldn't sleep. Deep sleep felt risky in a house filled with uncertainty and unknowns.

《 》

28

I've heard people talk about the circle of life. What goes around comes around and other such contiguous descriptions. But I think life is a seesaw, the kind that used to populate every children's playground. Seesaws rarely balance. They're usually in motion, either flinging you up or dropping you down. They can be fun or they can be terrifying—a lot of it depends on the other person.

If everyone cooperates, seesaws are terrific. But in my playground experience, just about the time you think you're having a great time riding to the top of the world, the other kid jumps off and you freefall until you hit the ground. The pain of the impact is shocking and terrifying.

My family's freefall from happy family to suicide survivors was as terrifying as any experience I can imagine. We felt copious amounts of regret—for not recognizing the signs of Charlie's depression, for having no magic solutions for Jen and the kids, for being so pitiful and helpless.

There were thousands of questions that begged for answers: Why didn't we know? Why didn't Charlie get help? What if he'd succeeded in killing himself? How could he do something that drastic? Didn't he love his kids and Jen? Could we ever trust him again? The questions floated in suspension during the first couple of weeks while we circled around Jen's family like a flock of protective geese and concentrated on survival.

Austin called around noon on January second and left a voicemail. We'd had such a wonderful time on New Year's Eve, I couldn't just drop off the planet without telling him, so I called him back that night after the kids had gone to bed and I could carve out a few minutes of privacy. After the initial shock, he was filled with concern for my family and me. He offered help or space, whichever I wanted. I opted for space. I was certain this was a "family-only" situation. Deep inside me, I didn't want to involve Austin in our family trauma. I wanted to keep our relationship unsullied and untainted; it was too young and fragile to be exposed. I figured after a couple of weeks, things would return to normal and Austin and I would pick up where we'd left off.

I stayed in Jen's guestroom until the middle of the second week when she felt stable enough for me to return home. Mom and Dad took over the errands Jen delegated to them—family laundry, grocery shopping, and the minor repairs that seemed to crop up at this most inopportune time—doing their work quietly while the kids were at school like elves in a fairy tale.

While we cared for Jen's family, each of us coped in our own way. My mother and father found comfort in their faith; although, that surprised me. I knew enough about the church of my Christmas and Easter holidays to know a suicide attempt doesn't get the same reaction as cancer or heart disease. People don't show up with casseroles and condolence cards after a suicide attempt. But my parents were fortunate to have good friends, deephearted people who didn't care if your particular family crisis was spiritually inconvenient. They listened without judging and supported without intruding. After their visits and phone calls, my mother folded laundry and my father sat outside and petted the dog without saying a word.

As for me, this was the first real family crisis I'd ever faced, and I found it incredibly disturbing. You may call me pampered, protected, sheltered. To a large extent, I was. The worst grief I'd ever faced before Charlie's suicide attempt was the death of my grandmother who had been eighty-nine years old and seriously ill. It was an expected funeral—hardly a crisis.

Now I was face to face with a truly terrifying family situation. At first, I'd pushed down my own thoughts and needs to care for Jen's family, but after I returned home, week three hit hard. My brain would not rest. I kept thinking round the clock—standard operating procedure for my brain under stress. Kick it into overdrive: analyze, dissect, examine, and conclude. My condo provided distance from the epicenter of the crisis so there were unlimited opportunities to think.

Thinking exposed emotion, and, like the rumblings of an unstable fault before an earthquake, I began to feel visceral anger. Not rock-crushing anger, just irritating thoughts that I didn't expect or want. I suppose anger is one stage of grief, and I should have known it would appear at one point or another. I had a history of being irritated by Charlie; anger was just the next step. The problem was, anger came coupled to another emotion: guilt. Feeling anger toward Charlie made me feel like the biggest jerk on the planet. Logically, I knew depression was an illness. Logically, I knew Charlie must have been seriously depressed. Logically, I knew all of that, but it didn't stop me from being angry.

Charlie's actions had taken our normal middle-class family and thrown us into turmoil. I'd never experienced this level of family turmoil before, and I didn't like it. It was like living in a witches' brew of guarded words, tears, sleeplessness, and pain that was impossible to escape.

Besides that, as much as I didn't want to face or admit it, Charlie's actions had changed my sister. Jen was struggling for control over her life, fighting to regain normalcy and balance, and it had destabilized my world. Jen had always been a rock of stability and predictability for me. Now she had become as unpredictable and moody as a tiger, always on alert, never fully trusting, protecting her den.

Jen was looking to me for comfort, stability, strength. I had little to give her since I was feeling off-balance myself. Austin and I talked every few days. Usually he called me, and more often than not our conversations were short. There were too many emotions to suppress, too many tasks to complete, too few words to provide meaningful explanation. Small talk was impossible, and deep conversations were time-consuming.

Infrequently, we would carve out enough time for a truly deep conversation. He would drive over and walk around the neighborhood with me, holding my hand and attentively listening. His words were comforting, but we didn't have enough shared history to support them and allow them to rise above my ground-floor struggles. Sometimes it felt like talking to a stranger. A kind, concerned stranger—but a stranger. I've never been much of a loner, but I found myself longing for time alone.

Saturday morning coaxed me out of bed as soon as the light hit my windows. I'd been feeling the pull of the Pacific for days, so I grabbed a quick bite of breakfast and drove the thirty minutes to the beach. It was a cool, overcast day. There were only a few cars parked along Coast Highway as I pulled into a space and slipped on my jacket.

Some beaches are perfect for surfing. Others are ideal for collecting shells and flying kites. My favorite beach is perfect for walking and running. There's always space between the sandstone bluffs and the high tide mark, space for running without the intrusion of an errant wave.

High tide had already drenched the sand, and small flocks of sandpipers darted along the shoreline looking for slow-digging sand crabs. Sandpipers are perfect running companions since they always seem to be running too. They're energetic and adorable, a winning combination in my book.

In times of uncertainty, I've always found the ocean comforting: the sounds of the waves, the smell of the clean salty air, the visual of all that blue expanse. I needed comfort that morning, some stability and security, and I needed some control over my untamed thoughts. Somehow I knew that being near something as large and powerful as the ocean would help put my thoughts into perspective.

The feel of my shoes against the sand was incredibly reassuring: rhythmic, predictable, solid. I ran the first half mile without thinking, just listening to the sound of the waves and the rhythm of my feet. One by one, the sounds were replaced by fleeting thoughts.

The memory of Jen's phone call loitered in my mind then vanished suddenly as I watched a surfer paddle out and catch a wave. I thought of that first week at Jen's house—the sleep deprivation, the fear, the uncertainty. I saw a mental picture of Jen, her hands wrapped around a cup of tea late one night and her eyes red from crying. I thought of Charlie and his behaviors during the past few months: isolation, moodiness, lack of interest, lethargy, detachment. My mind lingered on Charlie sitting in my parents' living room during the holidays, alone and withdrawn.

And then it hit me. Like a malfunctioning car, Charlie had been sending out signals, making noises, for a long time. In the last six months the intensity had increased to the point we couldn't ignore it. But like inexperienced mechanics, our diagnostics were all wrong. We thought his steering was malfunctioning when in fact his engine was falling apart.

I started thinking about the cocky, arrogant Charlie I'd judged and disliked so many years ago. Charlie had been abrasive, always determined to show his intellectual superiority, determined to get attention. And then another startling thought:

Maybe cocky and arrogant are signs of insecurity and internal pain.

Maybe Charlie had been sending signals for years, and we didn't recognize them.

I stopped running for a moment and looked out over the wide expanse of ocean. My mind was flooded with memories—conversations at my parents' house that used to irritate me because Charlie had to have the last word, had to be the expert.

Suddenly I remembered a powerful detail. My dad rarely challenged Charlie's conclusions or engaged in the heated debates. Why? Why didn't my dad challenge him, cut him down to size? Why didn't my dad insist on proving he was the smarter man, the alpha male in the room? Did my dad understand something about Charlie the rest of us had missed?

Those questions followed me as I ran back to my car. I grabbed my cell phone and called Dad.

"Dad," I said him after the expected how-are-yous. "Did you know something might be wrong when Charlie was dating Jen, when he acted so superior and arrogant all the time? Did you think he might have deeper issues...is that why you never put him in his place?"

"Oh, honey," Dad sighed. "Don't give me more credit than I deserve."

"What do you mean?"

"I knew Charlie was a young buck," Dad said. "To some extent most men are arrogant, otherwise they'd never have the courage to take on responsibility and become competent husbands. And honestly most men are relatively insecure in their twenties. They still have a lot to learn and they know it.

"But, to answer your question—no, I didn't realize the extent of Charlie's internal pain or know he was susceptible to depression."

"Oh," I said.

"I just knew he wanted to look smart and amazing to your sister, and I had no reason to deny him that."

I smiled. It was just like my dad to allow someone else to have the spotlight.

"So you didn't foresee that arrogant Charlie might someday become depressed Charlie?" I asked.

"No, I didn't," Dad replied. "If I'd been that wise, I would have done everything possible to protect your sister and intervene earlier. I only wish I'd been that astute. All I knew at the time was he had a lot to learn and life would probably take care of his arrogance."

I nodded even though he couldn't see me.

"Dad," I said softly. "Did you ever feel that level of insecurity? Have you ever dealt with deep depression?"

I heard Dad sigh.

"No, honey, I can't honestly say I've ever felt seriously depressed," he said. "My personality tends to see the glass as half full most of the time."

He paused for a moment, thinking, and then continued.

"Like most men I've felt worry, fear, and even a sense of helplessness. Life can feel overwhelming at times, and that creates personal doubts and worry, especially when you're responsible for a wife and kids. But to completely lose hope, to feel life isn't worth living—that's something I haven't felt before. That's why this situation with Charlie has hit me very hard because I didn't know he was depressed or suicidal. I didn't see it coming."

"Me either," I said. "None of us did, did we?"

"No, none of us did," Dad said. The sadness in his voice made the phone feel heavy in my hand.

"How could we have missed the signs?" I asked softly, even though I instinctively knew my dad's wisdom would fall short of a concrete answer.

Dad sighed. "I've asked myself that question a hundred times," he responded. "I don't know." There was a long pause before he continued. "I just don't know."

I looked out over the ocean for a moment and let silence fill the gap in our conversation. This was the most sadness I'd ever heard from my dad. His pain was palpable.

"Are you all right, Dad?" I asked.

"Sure, honey. I'm all right," he answered quickly, almost reflexively. Then the tone of his voice changed again and the sadness reappeared. "It's just so hard on your sister and your mother, not to mention the kids, Charlie, you..." His voice dropped off suddenly. I could tell his voice was following his mind down a path where hacking through the emotional underbrush made conversation impossible. Dad was quiet for a few moments. I thought he would finish his sentence, but he never did.

"I love you, Dad," I said, realizing there was only one way to graciously end the conversation. "I'll see you and Mom this week."

"Love you too, baby. Call me anytime."

After we hung up, I sat in my car looking out the window. The sun glistened across the tops of the waves creating an explosion of brightness and color. A lone surfer, sealed in a dark gray wetsuit, walked toward the beach with a long board under his arm. An old memory flashed through my mind. I was back at work watching quietly as my friend Dave grieved for his mother. I'd tried to reach out to him, tried to give him a reason to notice the light and beauty around him, but he walked alone in his grief.

I'd watched Charlie drift away from Jen as he tried to single-handedly cope with increasing stress and depression. And now I'd just seen my dad's retreat to his own thoughts when I got too close to a core regret—his inability to predict and prevent pain within his family.

Of all the things I'd learned from men, the hardest one to understand was their default into isolation. Throughout my life I'd seen the same pattern over and over. Isolation seemed to be one part of the male gene code that carried good men away, especially at times when they needed support the most.

≪ ≫

29

All my thinking at the beach had brought on an insatiable desire to know more about the connection between male depression and isolation. I decided to do a little Internet surfing late that night when sleep mysteriously vanished and wouldn't return.

Although I didn't identify with the isolation thing, I figured I already knew most of what anyone was going to say about depression. After all, I'd had PMS a few times too many. I'd broken up with boyfriends and wished I could crawl into a cave and die. If a break-up isn't the most depressing thing on the planet, I don't know what is.

The first website was filled with statistics. Frankly it was like reading a statistic textbook, and after the first year of my master's program, I'd had enough statistics to last a lifetime, so I kept surfing.

It didn't take long to find a site devoted to personal stories. One caught my attention. It was the story of a New York firefighter, Jimmy Brown, who struggled with depression for months after 9/11. He was used to being the strong one in any situation, so facing his growing despondency and seeking help for depression were as foreign to him as approaching the makeup counter at Nordstrom.

Jimmy was openly sharing his experience as part of a National Institute of Mental Health campaign called "Real Men. Real Depression." He was in good company. A lawyer, a publisher, a college student, a retired Air Force sergeant, and a national diving champion all put their stories out on the web to help other men identify, understand, and treat depression.

I sat reading for over an hour. There was page after page of personal accounts, quotes that told haunting stories of isolating and personal pain. Finally I leaned my head back and sighed so deeply it surprised me. Deep inside me, I felt for these men.

It's bad enough as a woman to feel a little depressed and to understand it's hormones and given a couple of days it'll pass. All my girlfriends and I have dealt with that, and it sucks. But what I was reading didn't even compare. It was like comparing the ripples in a pool to a tidal wave. Men were drowning in depression, and according to every site I saw, for the most part, they were drowning alone.

I went back to the statistics page.

- For every two victims of homicide in the United States there are three deaths from suicide.
- There are now twice as many deaths due to suicide than due to HIV/AIDS.
- Over half of all suicides occur in adult men, aged twenty-five to sixty-five.

I re-read the last statistic again and again, and all I could think of was, "We nearly lost Charlie."

As much as Charlie had irritated me over the years, I couldn't imagine our family without him. Even worse, I couldn't imagine Jen as a widow, dealing with the horrible guilt of hating her husband for having an affair then realizing too late she'd misread all the signs of depression. That would be unbearable.

I thought of Blake and Sophie standing over their dad's grave, trying to make sense of something their minds weren't capable of understanding. Frankly, even as an adult I was having a hard time wrapping my mind around this level of depression. To me it seemed the Internet descriptions were a valiant attempt, but honestly, how can you make someone understand something they've never come close to experiencing? I could read the words, but I couldn't fully understand the suffering.

Apparently thousands of men were suffering in silence, just like Charlie, yet few people were talking about it. Our family sure wasn't. We were an amazing support team for each other, trying to regain stability and security. But we weren't talking about depression.

Very few people outside our family even knew about Charlie's suicide attempt. After all, it was perfectly fine to go back to the office after two weeks of sick leave and tell everyone you'd had bacterial pneumonia or abdominal surgery. But how was Charlie supposed to walk back into the office and announce he'd been in intensive therapy following a suicide attempt? Yeah, right. Especially not with rumors of layoffs and downturns in his industry.

So like a good family, we huddled and protected. Everyone seemed to intuitively understand the script and we stuck to it—Charlie just wasn't feeling well. It was the male version of "nothing to worry about, just female problems."

So why didn't we talk about depression?

Probably for the same reason women in the workplace are careful to downplay their menopausal symptoms. Male depression and female menopause—both great excuses for the HR department to say, "We'd better keep our options open because this employee might not be well enough for the job. We might not be able to count on them showing up in top form everyday."

The odd thing was, it seemed all right (even expected) for women to have a little depression now and then. I grew up knowing I'd have periods and they might come with bloating, cramps, and low-grade depression. I learned that from my mother, my sister, and my sixth-grade sex education class. Even my boyfriends and employers seemed to understand and accept that women had emotions, and depression was one of them. But all sex ed class said about guys was that they grew body hair, became aggressive, and thought about sex every three and a half minutes.

I don't remember a single time before Charlie's suicide attempt that I heard anything about men and depression. Unless you count the time my cousin Jack failed his bar exam for the second time. My mother got off the phone with my aunt, came into the living room, and told my dad, who simply said, "That's too bad." That was it. My aunt talked with my mom a few times in the months after. They'd talk about Jack's moodiness and the concern that he couldn't make enough money to support his wife and baby. But no one ever mentioned the word "depression."

Somehow, depression was always associated with women, hormones, periods, and, frankly, women being a little too emotional about the stresses of life.

Unless one of my uncles or cousins was hospitalized or very old, I rarely heard about men being anything but "fine"—as in, "How's Uncle Frank doing?"

"Oh, he's fine."

In my world, men were the rocks of the family. Now I realized men could experience painful debilitating emotions and severe depression. They could cross the line from "a little down" to clinical depression without obvious symptoms and without sharing it with their doctors or their loved ones.

The more I thought about it, the more it made sense. No one can be a rock all the time.

≪ ≫

30

I didn't have to think hard to find a real-life example of what I'd just read about men and painful emotions.

Ed Morton and his wife, Darlene, are friends of mine. I met them within eight hours of moving in when they showed up that first evening with a container of chicken noodle soup and a small bag of homemade cookies.

"You won't have time to cook tonight," Darlene had said as she pressed the food into my hand.

She and Ed introduced themselves, and as soon as they determined I was single, they gave me their phone number in case I ever needed anything—anything at all. It was a sweet old-fashioned gesture, and I adored them immediately.

Ed is actually Retired Colonel Edward Morton, a former army man who has traveled the globe and who lost his first wife to cancer. He and Darlene liked each other in high school, re-discovered each other at their fortieth reunion, and were married as soon as their grown kids could adjust to the idea. Their story could make anyone believe in miracles and the power of love.

Ed and Darlene were regulars on the sidewalk outside my window. Sometimes on beautiful sunny spring days when I would go for a run in our neighborhood or walk to the store I'd see them out strolling, holding hands as though they couldn't stand the idea of letting go. We would talk a little and wish each other well. Then one day, I realized I hadn't seen them on the sidewalk for quite a while. I dug out their phone number and called.

Ed answered the phone and with deep sadness in his voice told me Darlene had been hospitalized with a stroke.

It's times like this I'm glad to be my mother's child. I knew exactly what to do. The next day after work I cooked up some food, wrote out a card, and took both next door. Ed graciously accepted my offerings and told me Darlene was in bed. I realized then the days of Ed and Darlene strolling together were over.

From time to time I would see Ed pushing a wheelchair around the block. It was impossible to recognize Darlene. She was a shell of her former self, gaunt and stiff. Ed spoke tenderly to her, patted her hand, and made sure the sun didn't shine into her face.

He hired a day nurse to help him care for her, but after a few months, I saw an ambulance arrive silently and load Darlene into the back. Ed stood watching then got into his car and followed. He had made the difficult decision to move Darlene to an assisted living center.

Ed and I talked a few times after that in the late afternoons of summer while he tended the patio roses and I leaned over the fence. He was plagued with sadness, haunted by his own inability to protect and care for the woman he loved.

"I used to command an entire brigade, and now I can't even take care of my own wife," Ed lamented one evening as we stood talking over his gate. "I feel more helpless than I've ever felt before. It's a horrible feeling."

That conversation stuck in my mind for days—the hopelessness in his voice, the unspoken yet palpable grief of circumstances beyond his control.

Since then, I've watched Ed change. Week after week, he drives out in the morning and returns in the evening, faithfully sitting at Darlene's bedside as her heart continues beating. You might not say Ed is depressed, but I would. He still stands erect, the result of military training. He still eats and exercises and sleeps. He goes through the motions of living, but the life has gone out of his eyes. He is watching his wife's death march, and he can't stop it.

One evening, I sat at my window and watched Ed from a distance as he tended his roses. Ed was teaching me, and finally I was beginning to understand the lesson.

As a man, Ed longs to provide stability, tenderness, and security for Darlene. But life is denying him that opportunity, and he is trapped. He's as trapped as his wife and men don't do very well when they're trapped in a set of circumstances they cannot change or control. I was beginning to realize how important it was for men to feel some control over the trajectory of their lives. Take away their ability to influence the outcome through their own actions and they feel helpless and depressed.

Come to think of it, women feel that way too.

It wasn't rocket science, but I suddenly identified with Ed. We were both in a set of circumstances beyond our control. Everything affected us, but right now our actions affected very little. Or at least it seemed that way.

I wanted to scream and run away. Instead I got into the shower and let the hot water stream over my neck and back. Hot water soothed me.

By the time I got out of the shower, I was resolute. You can surround me with sadness and tragedy. You can make me face the reality that tragedy can and probably will happen in my life. But I will fight the feeling of helplessness as long as I'm alive. I will take action as long as I can, and I will choose to believe my actions can make a difference.

After I dried off and dressed, I cut a few clusters of grapes off the bunch on my countertop, put them on a plate surrounded by mini muffins, and took them over to Ed's house.

≪ ≫

31

I called Jen the next morning. It was Sunday. She sounded tired.

"Hey, I know you have a lot on your plate right now, but could you get away for a little breakfast?" I asked.

"That sounds really good," Jen said. "Let me see how Charlie is doing and see if the kids will be okay for the next hour or so. I'll call you right back."

We met at our favorite breakfast spot, hugged for nearly a minute, and found a table outside that looked like the perfect spot for private conversation.

"You doing all right?" I asked. "You must be exhausted."

"I'm doing okay I guess," Jen said. "I keep trying to figure out how to survive the next day and keep life normal for the kids.

"This whole thing is so surreal," she continued. "I still can't believe it. My husband has clinical depression, I'm in weekly therapy, my world has fallen apart." Tears formed in her eyes but held their ground until she brushed them away. "I can't believe this," she said, dabbing her eyes with her napkin.

"Me either," I said. "I've been doing a lot of reading on the Internet about male depression, and it's brutal."

"We weren't very prepared for this, were we?" Jen said suddenly. "We grew up believing if you work hard, do the right thing, eat right and exercise, and marry a good guy, you'll have a great life. I never figured I'd be the one to face a family crisis."

I sat there helplessly watching my sister as tears formed in her eyes. All I could do was touch her hand. After a minute, she rubbed the mascara from below her eyes.

"I guess I just have to play the cards I'm dealt," she said. "But I can't seem to figure out whether to call or bluff or fold. It's all too complicated."

I sat there for a minute, deciding if I should broach the subject. Jen saw the question in my eyes.

"What?" she asked.

"I don't know how to ask this," I said. "It's a tough question to put out there, and..." I hesitated. "It might hurt."

"Probably not more than anything we've already dealt with," Jen said. She had a point.

"Okay, well...I was just wondering..." I hesitated again. "I've felt a lot of different emotions since the thing with Charlie happened. Some I expected, some I didn't." I looked carefully to see if Jen had flinched. She hadn't.

"Sometimes," I said softly. "I even feel anger, which makes me feel guilty." I stopped and looked at my sister. Jen's eyes glistened with unreleased tears. "How about you?" I asked.

"You have no idea," she said. "The dominant emotions in my life right now are sadness, anger, and fear."

"Really?" My voice was tinged with relief. "I thought maybe I was the only one dealing with bits of anger."

"I'm dealing with it like you can't believe," Jen said, shaking her head. "Sometimes in the evening, when I'm so exhausted I can barely move, when I'm getting the kids ready for bed and cleaning up the kitchen and paying the bills and trying to pull together a major event for a client I can't afford to lose, I look over at Charlie and feel waves of anger. It doesn't last for long, but the feelings are there. Sometimes I feel anger that I'm carrying the whole family on my shoulders. Other times I'm angry because he's changed my world from predictable to unpredictable, from secure to unstable.

"I know it's not his fault," she continued. "But I didn't expect this from him. I thought I could always depend on him. Now I don't know what to think and that just sends me careening between anger and fear."

I looked at the anxiety in Jen's face. My question had clearly opened a vault of emotion that was painful and difficult.

"When you got married," I told her, "I thought Charlie would always be the guy who provided for you, who was the strong shoulder to lean on, who could be counted on to be like…" I stopped for a moment and looked directly at Jen. "Like Dad."

Jen looked down at her hands. The fingers of her right hand were tracing the grain in the wooden table. Over, across, around. "Yeah," she said. "I thought Charlie would always be there for me like Dad was for Mom. Charlie seemed like a strong man who could lead a family through anything. He talked like a leader. He acted so strong and so capable. I never thought he would…"

She stopped. Her hands dropped into her lap. "I feel so guilty for feeling any negative emotion toward him," Jen said. "He's hurting so badly."

"I know," I agreed. "I've been reading all about male depression on the web and thinking about guys I know who have faced tough times, and for the most part, I get their pain. But I'm having trouble accepting that men can't be strong all the time. It's hard to wrap my mind around the concept."

"I know," Jen said. "It's so unreasonable, but I still want to believe it."

"I feel like I'm learning an entirely new way of viewing men," I said. "I'm being forced to admit they have illogical emotions and instability sometimes, just like women. I wasn't prepared to think of them that way."

"Me either," Jen said. "I definitely wasn't prepared to find my husband attempting suicide and dealing with this level of depression." Both of us sat quietly for a moment, lost in our own thoughts and watching the server as he placed our food on the table. Suddenly Jen looked up and said, "I wonder if there's an *Idiot's Guide to Your Husband's Depression?*"

Her comment made us both laugh, which felt like the beginning of a bridge across a chasm. We could still laugh, even in the midst of conflicting emotions.

"I can't remember the last time I laughed," Jen said. "Obviously before …"

"Yeah, I know."

Shattering sounds made everyone turn and look. Glass and coffee spread all over the floor, a mess of brown and cream and debris. Patrons at the nearest table were standing to brush coffee off their clothes before the stains set in and restaurant staff were rushing to clean up. A single server stood apologizing red-faced to patrons at the table. Feeling the discomfort of everyone in the area, we turned back to our own conversation.

"I think Charlie feels like that," Jen said a moment later. "Embarrassed, humiliated."

"It must be hard to know the entire family has their eyes on you," I said.

We both looked away for a moment, lost in our own thoughts about mistakes, accidents, changed reality. And again I realized, once the damage is done, it's permanent. There's no going back.

"I'm really glad you called," Jen said after we paid the bill and began walking to our cars. "Thanks for figuring out a way for us to talk…just the two of us."

"I needed it," I told her as I reached for another hug. "There's so much going on, and I don't want to lose what we've always had."

"Me either," she said as she held me close to her.

Driving home, I listened to music for a few minutes, thinking about the waiter, the spilled coffee, Charlie. I absent-mindedly changed the station to NPR. *All Things Considered* was running a story about subtle prejudice and hidden bigotry. A bigot, the reporter said, is a person who holds blindly to a particular opinion about others that often negates or ignores the reality of the other person's pain or fear. That definition roamed around my brain as I drove.

Then suddenly, without warning, the diverse thoughts in my brain came together in an unexpected wave of self-realization.

I was a bigot. My mother, Jen, and most of my girlfriends were too. Our bigotry didn't relate to skin color or religion or appearance; we'd confronted those in childhood and divested ourselves of them. But in their place, we'd developed our own subtle prejudice against men.

Men were expected to be capable and strong, fearless and stable. They were expected to understand and meet our emotional needs, to comfort us and care for us without showing too much emotion in the process. Subtly, unconsciously we'd sent the message that they should take care of us but handle their own fears, embarrassments, and failures alone.

Like all well-developed bigotry, mine had allowed me to bunch men into simplistic categories like stable family man, inveterate womanizer, or clueless buffoon. TV had reinforced my stereotypes, and my father had been too non-confrontational to attack them. Maybe the isolation I'd witnessed in men wasn't just a byproduct of their gene code; maybe it was also a product of my unwillingness to let them be anything but single-dimensional and rock solid.

Women like me didn't want to acknowledge that our rocks had cracks—tiny cracks of real emotion. It was more convenient for us to ignore those microscopic cracks. More convenient and much safer because we knew given the right amount of pressure applied in just the right way, those cracks would break everything wide open and our sense of security would vanish.

Our bigotry toward men was based in our need for security. Even a false sense of security was better than none.

≪ ≫

32

It took about six weeks for our family to begin feeling anything close to normal again. During that time we all dealt with a range of emotions—denial, sadness, anger, compassion, fear, acceptance, then sadness again.

I spent as much time as possible with Blake and Sophie, trying to shore up the damaged wall of security and stability that had previously defined their world as normal.

"Daddy isn't feeling well right now," Jen had told them initially. The kids accepted her words as if Charlie had the flu. They asked few questions and seemed oblivious, just as they had seemed oblivious when Charlie's behavior became concerning. Jen always seemed to have age-appropriate answers to their infrequent questions. She confided that many of her answers came from Dr. Neval. That was reassuring to both of us.

Blake and Sophie were used to me being around the house, so it didn't unnerve them when I made dinner for the family or helped them into bed. In fact, they seemed to enjoy the attention they were receiving from my parents and me. Mom and Dad took care of them a few days a week until I got off work, then I took over and supported Jen in the evenings and on weekends. When Jen and Charlie went to appointments, the kids and I went to the park. When Jen was too tired to help with homework, Sophie and I sat in the family room and practiced simple addition while Blake filled in worksheets, his forehead furrowed in concentration and his fingers continually adjusting the grip on his pencil.

I'd always loved my niece and nephew, but now my love for them had developed into something deeper. I felt compelled to meet their needs, at times even more than I felt compelled to meet Jen's. They were far too young and unprepared for the harsh reality of their changed world. I know the concept of a "mothering instinct" is controversial, but there was no denying it. Mine kicked in with a vengeance. I stepped into a nurturing, mothering role toward Blake and Sophie as naturally as if I'd given birth to them. Nothing trumped their needs, not Jen's, not Charlie's, not even my own.

It was the right thing to do, but it left me exhausted. I had to jettison the extras in my life. My condo became cluttered, and my exercise routine deteriorated to nothing. My relationship with Austin suffered the most.

Austin and I were still dating, if you can call infrequent phone calls and even more infrequent time together dating. He'd done his best to be supportive during the last six weeks without making me claustrophobic. He listened when I talked. The problem was, I was so absorbed with Jen's situation, I had little time or energy to offer him.

Looking back, I'm not sure why Austin stuck with me through all this, but he did, even when I wasn't fully present. He just kept calling or texting periodically and came over when I invited him, which wasn't often.

"I know you're busy," he'd say at the beginning of any phone call. "But could you get away for dinner tonight?"

"I'm so sorry," I would answer more often than not. "I promised to take the kids for pizza after work" or "Blake has a project due, and Jen is too tired to help him."

"I miss you," Austin would say. "I hope your sister's family is doing better."

"It's going to take a long time, but I think they're on the right track," I'd reply. "Sorry—I have to run."

Like all good men, Austin didn't make too much of it. He just kept himself busy and stood quietly by while I sorted out my emotions, supported my sister, and spent time with my niece and nephew. I knew he'd be all right, so I didn't worry. But I did miss him.

≪ ≫

33

One cool day in mid-February, Mom invited all of us to dinner. My parents had finally found their footing and realized we needed more time together as a family. The glue that held our family close refused to let go under the pressure.

Charlie had been doing his work, keeping his appointments, following his doctor's orders, slowly opening up and talking to Jen. Although he and I had been in the same household many times since "that night," I hadn't talked with Charlie much. He was usually at work or upstairs in the bedroom. As I began to think about dinner, I realized Charlie was an unknown to me now. I might have pieced together a few pieces of the puzzle by reading and thinking, but the main piece, the reality of who Charlie was at this moment in time, was still missing.

Long ago, I had accepted the arrogant Charlie; although, I didn't really like him. He was a known part of our family. I had faced the wayward Charlie and was fully prepared to testify against him at the divorce proceedings. But this Charlie...the Charlie of vulnerability, depression, and healing...this Charlie was alien to me. It was unnerving. I was filled with compassion from a distance but hesitant to actually face him at a family dinner.

I woke at four a.m., stared at the ceiling for twenty minutes, then decided to go for a run. Exercise had become an occasional extravagance over the last two months, and I missed my routine.

It was calm and quiet on the street. An occasional car sped by, driven by someone who knew this early hour better than me. This time of morning was a mystery to me. Even the sun wasn't familiar with four a.m. And because it was so unfamiliar out here on the street at that hour, I found myself aware of small things. The traffic signal colors were bold with early morning moisture, a dog barked in the distance, home irrigation systems turned on and off as I passed. I ran for nearly three miles and came home tired. I thought briefly of calling Austin before work. By the time I showered, it was too late.

I probably should have asked Austin to come to our family dinner, but I didn't. It felt like my family needed to be alone together, just us facing our changed reality. I still cared for Austin, maybe I'd even started to love him at some point before everything broke loose, but now our conversations felt dry and predictable. The flame between us was barely flickering. So I didn't ask him to come to dinner. We didn't even talk that day.

It was a challenging day at work, and I was ready to leave quickly. Fortunately nothing prevented that. Even the chatty woman in the next office seemed intent on getting out of the building, so we both just smiled and left without a forced conversation. I rushed home, changed out of my skirt, and let my mind wander as I drove. I tried listening to the radio, but my thoughts always defaulted to Sophie and Blake, Jen and Charlie. I couldn't stop thinking about them. It was as if they'd moved into my brain and squeezed out thoughts of anyone else.

Mom answered the door dressed in a pink sweater and gray pants. She looked elegant and beautiful, the picture of a mother whose children were all successful and well placed. You could only see the stress of the last six weeks by looking into her eyes. Two months before they'd sparkled with life, but now they looked tired and sad. She hugged me close as Dad came around the corner.

"Hi, sweetie," Dad said. "I'm so glad you're here."

"It smells good in here," I said as I hugged him.

The smell of garlic, beef, and orange all mixed together to create an aroma of familiarity. I recognized the smells of my favorite garlic potatoes, Jen's favorite prime rib, and Dad's favorite orange cake. Dad had a fire in the fireplace that made comforting crackling noises as I walked through the living room into the kitchen where Mom had started slicing cucumber into the salad. Charlie and Jen hadn't arrived yet.

I looked around and suddenly felt the warmth and comfort of my final years at home alone with my parents. There were just a few years between the time Jen left home and my departure—years of special memories: silly fights over curfews and dirty clothes on the floor, college applications at the kitchen table, whispered goodnights from my parents' bedroom when I tiptoed past after midnight.

They were good people, my parents. Good people who refused to surrender their family to a crisis. Leaders who were prepared to muster their team after a devastating loss. As I looked across the kitchen at their lined faces, I realized they were going to do it. They were going to guide us as we searched for something to reconnect our family and create a whole again. Until they knew exactly what that was, they were going to serve food and make fires in the fireplace.

The doorbell rang, and I was surprised to feel my heart rate jump. I wanted to greet Jen at the door, yet I wanted to stay in the kitchen. It was an odd mix of emotions.

I stood in the kitchen while Dad opened the front door. Mom wiped her hands on a towel and walked out of the kitchen without insisting I join her. It was my parents' way. To blaze a trail and let us follow when we were ready.

Jen found me in the kitchen minutes later. Without a word, she walked over and threw her arms around me. We held each other for a long time, feeling the warmth of sisterhood and savoring the smells of Mom's familiar kitchen.

"What can I do?" Jen asked, wiping the hair out of her face. "Does Mom need any help?"

"I don't know," I said. "I just arrived too."

Dad began talking with Charlie in the living room while the kids opened cabinets and retrieved remotes. My parents had bought an Xbox as soon as they realized it was a powerful incentive to inspire grandchildren's visits. Within minutes, the electronic sounds drifted from the TV into the kitchen.

"How are you doing, honey?" Mom asked Jen as she entered the kitchen.

"A day at a time," Jen responded. "It's a lot harder than I thought."

"I know," Mom said as she retrieved forks from the drawer. "Your dad and I pray for you everyday."

Jen nodded. "I appreciate that a lot."

Mom opened the oven door and, satisfied that the contents were ready, said, "Would you girls set the table for me?"

Jen and I carefully placed plates, silverware, glasses, and napkins on the table. The routine felt normal, even if our conversation was sparse. We had no trouble talking in private, but when there were others around, we watched our words. Within minutes, Mom was calling everyone to eat.

I hadn't seen Charlie in over a week, so I walked over to give him a hug before we sat down. I didn't expect him to look so exhausted. He'd obviously lost a little weight, but other than appearing tired and slightly thinner, Charlie looked pretty good. I hugged the kids and asked them about school and about the projects we'd worked on together. They seemed fine.

I'd love to say dinner was relaxed and pleasant, but that would be a lie. The food was delicious. My mother can cook her way through any occasion, and her recipes have an amazing capacity to soothe and warm you from the inside. Being together was the right thing. We needed each other, and we all knew it. But the conversation didn't flow. It was guarded. We all checked our words internally before letting them slip out of our mouths. It wouldn't be right to spoil the moment with a misplaced reference to guns or death or therapy or marriage or sadness or any number of other potential verbal grenades. So Dad stuck to topics like community events, jobs, and the kid's schoolwork—topics that were safe and felt a little empty.

Watching Charlie trying to act as if nothing had happened was almost a torturous as watching Jen trying to pick up the pieces of their formerly perfect lives and reassemble them into something that didn't appear broken. A quote kept popping into my mind as I watched them.

All marriages are happy. It's the living together afterward that causes all the trouble.

Raymond Hull said that. I can't remember when I first heard it, but probably in high school because my social sciences teacher was enamored with *The Peter Principle*, co-written by Lawrence Peter and Raymond Hull. My teacher was convinced it explained everything you needed to know about public education.

In previous family conversations, I might have made a point to verbalize this quote, to rub my knowledge in Charlie's face. But tonight, it didn't feel appropriate. Tonight, I had no desire to compete with Charlie. Our family had to band together. If living together causes all the trouble and if you're going to survive life, every marriage, every family has to find its own way to cope.

You can face life like rats on a treadmill, running hard and getting nothing but food, water, and toys; you can face it like survivors on an island, huddled together in fear waiting for the next big wave; or you can face it like arctic explorers, each member of the team bringing part of the gear and part of the knowledge so when you encounter the unexpected, between all of you, there are enough resources to survive.

I looked around the table and realized my family was a group of survivors. We'd make it. It might take months or even years, a lot longer than any of us had initially anticipated, but in the end we would bring the gear, share the knowledge, and survive.

≪ ≫

34

Austin and I had a very difficult talk in early March.

I knew things had deteriorated between us, largely due to my own inability to invest anything in our relationship. There were only so many hours in my day, and by the time I worked, supported Jen, nurtured the kids, talked with my mom or dad, ran errands, and gave my mind time to sort it all out, I was exhausted. Dealing with a family crisis has a way of pushing everything else to the side, forcing even the best relationships off the road and into the ditch.

I felt especially bad because Austin had tried so hard. He had called, sent texts, proposed dates. But I was too buried in my own family dynamic to give him anything in return.

Dating requires time, and I didn't have any extra. Dating requires emotional connection, and I didn't have any emotion to spare. Somehow I just couldn't find the strength to date anyone, and I reluctantly faced that fact one evening when Austin and Axle happened to be walking by my condo and I happened to be home.

"Are you home?" Austin texted when he was three blocks away.

"Yes."

"Can I drop by for a few minutes and talk?"

While Axle waited patiently on the grass, Austin and I sat in the chairs by my open window. Our conversation was brief and surprisingly void of strong emotion or acrimony.

"I'm not sure how to bring this up," Austin began, reaching for my hand. "I really care about you, and I'll be honest, I want to be with you, but..." He stopped short.

"I know," I said.

He waited a bit before continuing. "So, do you want to keep dating?" he asked. His eyes were sad, as if he already knew my answer.

I sighed and looked out the window for a few seconds. "I don't know," I said. "I'm just so tired all the time. I don't feel like I have any energy for anything."

"Look," Austin said. "I get it. Your family's going through a terrible time...I don't know all the details, but I know enough to understand this is really hard..." He and I were both looking out the window now even though there was nothing outside to merit our focus. His voice trailed off. I knew he was trying to find the appropriate words. I couldn't think of any either.

"You deserve better than I can give you right now," I offered.

"Is that your way of saying we should just be friends?"

"Maybe."

"Okay," he said. His head was nodding and the muscles in his jaw were tight. "Okay, then. Well, I should go. I've got an early meeting tomorrow. I'd better get home and get some sleep."

I nodded. My eyes reached out for his, and I gave him a weak smile. He smiled back. It was a lifeless smile, the kind you'd give a co-worker who might be in line for your job.

"I'm really sorry," I said as I followed him to the door.

"It's okay," he said. "I understand." We both knew he didn't. Frankly, neither did I.

And then he was gone.

I walked into my bedroom, turned on the TV, and lay down. There weren't any tears, just the noise of the TV and sad silence inside me. I woke up three hours later, turned off the TV, took off my make-up and clothes, and softly cried myself to sleep.

Breaking up had been harder than I thought it would be. I thought my feelings toward Austin were buried so deep under my family's problems that they wouldn't resurface. I was wrong. For a couple of weeks, I did little except work, sleep, watch TV, talk to Jen or the kids, and cry. I tried to stop thinking because frankly it was too hard to be alone with my thoughts. My brain would blenderize regrets and missed opportunities until they were a messy, foamy brew. I missed Austin, but I didn't have the energy to go after him and invite him back.

About three months after Charlie's suicide attempt, about the time spring appeared with its blossoms and bright green growth, I woke up one morning and realized it was time to move on. I'd cried my tears for Austin. It was a missed opportunity that simply wouldn't come around again. I had to accept that.

My life had become a dead planet orbiting around an old explosion. It was time for change. Not just a momentary change, but a rebirth. I needed to focus on something besides my sister's life. I loved her, but I had my own life to live and I was doing a poor job of it. If I didn't want to spend the next forty years at my desk or alone watching reality TV, I had to change.

Eating my way out of the mess was clearly going to be too fattening, so I decided to launch into a serious exercise routine. I'd gone running a few times in the months after Jen's discovery, but the last few weeks had been a lethargic zone. If all the women's magazines were true, exercise would make me a happier, healthier, and sexier woman in weeks. I just had to get off my self-pitying ass and get moving.

Running is a great time for self-evaluation. You can run away from lots of things, but your thoughts come along on every mile. I thought about Austin, I thought about Jen and her kids, I thought about my parents, I thought about everyone I loved or had loved.

For the first time, I started to see things I wanted to change about myself. In just a couple of years, I was going to be thirty. I couldn't escape the fact I'd become someone I wouldn't want to marry, someone I wouldn't want to be friends with. I'd become an unhappy woman smeared with the residue of lingering emotions and unanswerable questions. I had no social life, and my friends hadn't seen me in weeks—both unacceptable.

A few days after I began running, the endorphins kicked in. Actually, scientifically speaking, it probably wasn't just endorphins, but I sure felt better. I had more energy and didn't feel so pathetic. I actually wanted to do something besides cry, sleep, and watch TV.

I started by cleaning my condo, which I realized had begun to look uncharacteristically dirty. Cleaning is the ultimate therapy for me. You can have your health spas and herbal remedies. Give me Mr. Clean and a vacuum. The moment I start attacking dust and dirt, I feel strong, healthy, and empowered.

After my condo was clean, I decided to walk down to the market and pick up some decent food. My fridge was begging. It was a beautiful sunny day, the kind Midwesterners envy when spring is overdue. The sun warmed my face, the snapdragons stood at attention in patio pots, and everything seemed to warm my soul. I smelled mint and rosemary as I walked by one patio then roses as I passed Ed's. It was almost as though I was awake after a long, uncomfortable sleep.

I thought about the infamous grief timeline, how everyone has his or her own and how you can't rush it and best not avoid it. In the middle of grief and pain it feels like it will last forever. But when you finally break out of the fog, you suddenly have hope again. Hope that tomorrow could be a good day. Hope that the future could make you smile.

I wondered if Charlie had found hope yet. If his fog had lifted so he could look across the table at Jen and his kids and see all the reasons he wanted to live a long and happy life.

≪≫

35

Jen invited Mom, Dad, and me to dinner one cool evening in April. During my lunch break I decided to walk by my favorite bakery, and when I saw the black forest cake, I called Jen and offered to bring dessert.

Jen had warned all of us to expect a deep conversation. As part of his ongoing therapy, Charlie had decided to open up about his depression, to share more of his family history and insights he'd learned in therapy.

When I first heard the evening's agenda, I felt myself emotionally retract—the typical sea anemone response. Touch me in a vulnerable spot and my self-protection kicks in. I was in a good place emotionally, and I didn't want to risk a relapse. I didn't particularly want to talk about depression and pain. But after a few minutes of reflection, I realized listening and learning would be therapeutic for all of us. I wanted to be part of our family's healing, and I was interested to hear what Charlie had to say. Jen and I could conjecture; only Charlie could honestly and openly share what was going on inside his mind.

I arrived as Jen was loading the kids into her girlfriend Laurie's minivan. They were off for an evening of pizza and games with Laurie's family and would be home in three hours.

Dinner was simple and delicious. We talked about Mom and Dad's trip to Boston to see my Aunt Dottie. We talked about the upcoming election. We talked about the kids. It wasn't until after dinner, when we moved into the family room and settled into the leather, that Charlie cleared his throat to speak.

"I really don't know how to start this," he began. "I want to share some things with you, but I don't want to make you too uncomfortable or turn this evening into a downer."

"Charlie," Dad interjected. "We all know why we're together tonight. You don't have to mince words. We're here to listen." Dad reached for Mom's hand, and they held onto each other.

"Well," Charlie said. "I appreciate that. It's just hard to compress all my thoughts into coherent sentences."

"It's okay, son," Dad said.

"All right..." Charlie began. "You know I've been in counseling for over three months now. And I just want you to know it's helping. I'm starting to see patterns in my life that have contributed to my depression, and I'm starting to see it's important to share my feelings with those I love, especially Jen."

Dad nodded. I kept my focus on Charlie. He looked vulnerable yet somehow stronger than he'd looked a month ago. He looked more present. That was it—like he was actually in the room with us instead of miles away in a world of pain and exhaustion.

"I don't know if you've ever wondered why Jen and I spend most holidays with you and rarely visit my family. Well it's because my dad is an alcoholic. I'm never sure what I'll find if I go home for holidays, and I'm never sure if the kids will somehow discover their Gramps drinks too much.

"See, my dad was never an angry, mean drunk, so our family just ignored the problem. Dad would sometimes stay out too late and drink too much, but then he'd come home and go right to bed. My mom never talked about it, so we kids learned to ignore it. Frankly, I never thought it had any effect on me. It was just a little family secret we kept well hidden.

"Then about three years ago, my job started getting much more stressful. I knew Jen had a lot going on with her job and the kids. I didn't want to burden her, so sometimes in the afternoon I'd stop by a restaurant near work and have a couple of drinks, and then I'd go back to work for a few hours. It relaxed me, so I thought I'd found the perfect solution to my stress. It kept me from bringing my frustration home and kept me happy at the office. In my mind, it was a win-win situation, but I didn't realize it was actually playing into my genetic predisposition toward depression."

126

Charlie stopped. He looked at his hands for a moment then reached over toward Jen, who grasped one of his hands in both of hers.

"Obviously I didn't know I had any depression genes," Charlie said. "Only counseling has helped me identify my father's depression and quite a bit of depression in my mother's family. Anyway, as things got more and more stressful at work, I just kept drinking more and distancing myself from Jen and the kids so they wouldn't be able to tell. The last thing I wanted was to bring my stress home, and I knew if Jen smelled too much liquor on my breath, she'd start asking questions."

I looked at Jen. Her expression was held in place with resolve. I realized how hard it must be for her hear this from Charlie, although I was sure they'd already talked about it privately. It felt like Charlie was painting Jen as a strict and demanding wife, but as soon as this thought crossed my mind, Charlie reached over and pulled Jen closer to him. She didn't resist. Without hesitation, she reached up, put her hand over his as it lay across her shoulder, and squeezed for him to continue.

"It's obvious to me now that I made a huge mistake," Charlie said. "Pulling away from Jen and hiding this from her was one of the most isolating things I could have done, but at the time I just didn't see any other way to cope. That's the baffling thing about depression," Charlie continued. "It makes you feel like people won't understand, like they'll think you're stupid or inept."

"That would be very hard for a man," Dad said, looking directly at Charlie.

"Yes," Charlie replied, "very hard. So I just retreated into my own world of work and drinking. Then about a year ago, the pressure at work began building. Our margins were dropping, and new work stopped coming in the door. When I noticed the trends and started hearing everyone else talk about the downturn, I got really worried. I knew we couldn't pay the bills on Jen's income alone. There were rumors circulating about layoffs. My boss was getting surly, and no matter what I tried, it didn't change the bottom line.

"The pressure kept increasing last summer and got worse and worse through fall. By Thanksgiving, it was almost unbearable. You probably noticed I wasn't very happy during the holidays."

"Yeah," I said softly. "I wondered about that."

"Well, that's about the time I started thinking seriously about suicide. I felt like I was drowning at work and terribly distant from my family. Somehow in my mind it started to make sense that Jen would be better off if I was dead. With her income, she'd be able to have a good life and provide for the kids. To show you how messed up my thinking was, I even convinced myself she'd be happier and better off if I just died and gave her the chance to remarry someone else while she was still in her thirties."

Deep in my stomach, I felt a small wave of nausea. How was it possible for Charlie to believe Jen would be better off with him dead? I had a brief picture of Jen as a widow, greeting guests at Charlie's funeral. It was a horrifying thought. Even in my deepest pit of PMS, when I wanted to crawl under my covers and hide, I never believed my family would be better off if I was dead. I knew if anything bad happened to me, it would be devastating for them.

I looked over at Jen. She was brushing her eyes with the back of her hand trying not to cry. Mom was dabbing at her eyes. There was a lot of sympathy in the room. You could feel it, and it was strong enough to sustain Charlie as he continued.

"I wish now I would have shared these feelings of worry with Jen a lot earlier. It breaks my heart to think she believed..." Charlie's voice trailed off for a moment. It took him a minute to compose himself and continue. "Anyway, all of you know what happened in January. I don't think I have to go through that again, do I?"

"No, Charlie, we know that was your lowest point," Dad said kindly. "I would like to know how you're feeling about therapy and your future."

"Sure," Charlie said. "Well, I'm definitely learning a lot about myself in therapy. My family didn't have many healthy ways of coping with stress or disappointment. We mostly ignored anything that involved emotion, so I'm learning healthy techniques to cope with stress and acknowledge emotion. I'm also learning to trust Jen can handle things that are hard. It's not good for either of us if I hide my stresses or emotions from her."

Charlie paused, and Jen seamlessly carried his thought to the next level. "And I'm learning how to support him without mothering him," Jen offered. "My personality just wants to get in there and solve the problems, so I'm learning to back off a little and listen more, so he can talk without feeling like I'll demand a quick solution."

"Had you been interacting that way before?" Mom asked. "If that's not too personal a question."

"I didn't realize it, but yes," Jen answered. "I've had a tendency to listen for a few minutes then expect Charlie to come up with quick and effective answers to any problem. I didn't realize how much pressure that puts on him. How he felt he couldn't discuss anything with me unless he already had a solution figured out."

"That's a lot of pressure on a man," Dad said. "I know you didn't do it on purpose, honey."

"No, I didn't," Jen said. "But it had the same effect. I'm learning a better way of listening and supporting Charlie when things are stressful."

"And I'm learning better ways to support her," Charlie said. "After all, I'm not the only one who carries stress. Little by little, we're learning to be a team again."

"That's good to hear," Dad said.

"I just want to say one more thing," Charlie said. "I didn't realize how easy it is to feel overwhelmed and isolated…to carry stress that will eventually overwhelm me. And I didn't realize I had depression and drinking issues in my family that would take me to a point of suicide. But I realize all that now, and I'm committed to do whatever it takes so these things don't destroy Jen, the kids, and me. I love them too much to hurt them ever again.

"I might struggle with depression in the future, but I promise I won't try and face it down by myself anymore."

Jen squeezed Charlie's hand and looked at me. I looked at the pictures of the kids on the wall and looked at Mom. No one knew what to say. We wanted to be supportive, but we weren't quite sure what words to use.

"Do you have anything you'd like to ask me?" Charlie offered. "I understand I put everyone through a horrible experience, and I'm willing to answer any questions you ask…that is, if I know the answers."

Jen looked at me again, and I gave her a small smile. What was I supposed to say? All the questions previously generated by negative emotions had slowly receded. They didn't scream for answers from Charlie the way they once had. Now they simply sat in the corner waiting to be addressed in a gentler way.

"I do have one question, Charlie," I said after a few seconds. I briefly considered digging up an old question that started with "why" or "how could you" but realized they didn't seem appropriate in the current discussion. Charlie was a different man now. It was time to look forward instead of backward. "Is there anything Mom, Dad, or I can do as part of your therapy?" I asked. "I've felt really helpless in all this. Honestly, Charlie, I always cared, I just didn't know what to do except support Jen. So if there's a role for our extended family, a way we can directly show our support for you, I'd like to know what it is."

Jen gave me a look of gratitude. Mom and Dad looked relieved. Frankly those looks didn't matter as much as the feeling I had. Finally I had found the resources within myself to talk directly and honestly with Charlie. Conflicting emotions had subsided, and in their place I'd found compassion.

"I really appreciate that," Charlie said, looking directly into my eyes. "Right now, I'm still working on the early phases of therapy. But I think there may come a time when I'd like all of us to talk again. For now, would you just be sure to say something to me if you think I'm retreating into isolation? I don't want to go there again."

"Sure," I said. "I want you to know we love you and we're here for you."

That night I lay in bed for a while before I fell asleep. I kept thinking about men, depression, and isolation. It's not that women don't feel isolated sometimes. We do. But we're not afraid to use the d-word. We throw it around like a handbag. Honestly, if you want to hear about depression, go into any women's restroom and wait a few minutes. It's a common topic.

I got up, wrapped myself in flannel, and spent a few minutes online looking at sites about men and depression again. One quote stood out, written by a man who'd battled depression since his teens: "I would never say I was depressed to a friend because I'm not sure a guy would understand what I meant. It's just not an emotion most men understand, and we tend to avoid even the emotions we do understand."

I still didn't get it. I've never been hesitant to admit I'm slightly depressed to a girlfriend. It usually brings an offer of lunch, shopping, or chocolate. Although I've never experienced clinical levels of depression, I don't think I'd be afraid to ask for help if I did. But to men, it was an unspeakable topic. Something too risky to talk about.

Well, the world might not be talking about male depression, but my family had spent an evening discussing it, and somehow it felt like "the something" we'd been searching for. Talking together felt like opening a painful wound to fresh air and sunshine, an environment where healing could happen.

《》

36

It's interesting how families handle crises. After Charlie opened up and we each took time to absorb his words and integrate them into our view of our family unit, we began to find our equilibrium again, and our world began to feel like it was spinning on the correct axis. I'm honestly not sure whether that was a function of Charlie's honesty, Jen's admissions, our willingness to listen to each other, or what. I just know after that evening, something changed for the better.

We still guarded our words for a while. No reason to cause unnecessary discomfort. We still watched for signs that Charlie was becoming depressed again. We all knew it was not only a possibility, it was a statistical probability. For now, his doctor, therapist, and exercise routine all seemed to be keeping things in balance. I still found myself sliding back into the "whys" of the last six months, but those were relatively easy to discard, like an old pair of jeans that no longer fit.

I watched as Charlie and Jen slowly rebuilt their trust. Although Charlie hadn't had an affair as Jen had feared, he had managed to live a double life for nearly three years, hiding his afternoon drinking and his depression. So in an odd way, they still had to do the hard work of rebuilding trust. It wasn't easy for Jen. She had to cope with her own emotions and the realization she'd nearly lost her husband. She had to find a way to talk about feelings and stresses with a husband who was still prone to depression. Both of them still had to figure out how to handle the construction downturn as they paid their bills and raised their kids.

Watching them rebuild their marriage, I began to see a different side of my sister. Charlie wasn't the only vulnerable one. Jen was raw and vulnerable too. She'd been to the edge of an emotional cliff, and looking down into the abyss had changed her perspective. It wasn't like she'd lost her confidence or her strength, but she seemed more willing to acknowledge the gray areas of life. Her black-and-white world of quick solutions and efficient options had been replaced by a world of myriad colors and shaded resolution. Surprisingly it softened her. Instead of looking pathetic and victimized, Jen's vulnerability made her appear more real and sympathetic.

Little by little, family time started to feel familiar and comfortable again. It was the barometer by which I judged our family's internal pressure, and I continually monitored our time together. I knew we were going in the right direction by May. We celebrated Mother's Day together, and Charlie wrote beautiful words in the card about family love and support and how he couldn't have done it without my mother's prayers.

A few weeks later, we were all sitting together at Sophie's kindergarten graduation, trying not to laugh at the little boy on the back row who kept picking his nose as the teacher droned on about a year of intellectual growth and greater maturity. Looking down the row at each member of my family suppressing laughter, seeing the contented look on Dad's face, watching Mom squeeze Jen's hand as Sophie walked across the stage—these and other little gestures convinced me our family barometer was rising.

My personal barometer was rising too. I looked around the auditorium that evening as the kindergarteners and their families took pictures. A year ago, I would have been content to critique the women and categorize the men. Now I saw each family as a dynamic, intricate microcosm dealing with diverse emotions and challenges. A year ago, I might have been snickering about the woman with the out-of-date hairstyle and too-short pants. Now I was actually admiring the way she managed to sternly but lovingly keep her third grader in line with a simple glance while the rest of her beamed with pride over her graduating daughter. Her hair and clothes seemed irrelevant.

By the time Father's Day came around, we were all looking forward to the barbecue and the backyard water balloon fight, our family tradition. Charlie and Dad cooked the burgers and watched the kids. Mom, Jen, and I were in the kitchen slicing tomatoes and washing lettuce when Jen suddenly reached for Mom and me. Her touch instantly said more than "Have you seen the paring knife?" It was the touch of deep emotion, a touch from the center of her heart. She gathered both of us in her arms and pulled us in toward her.

"I can't thank you enough," she said with her face buried in my hair. "I couldn't have made it without you."

Neither Mom nor I said anything. We just stood there with our arms wrapped around each other, holding on like expedition survivors. Jen's hair felt soft against my face, and Mom's hand radiated warmth along the small of my back. After two or three minutes, we wiped our noses, dabbed our eyes, and started setting the table.

It wasn't that we didn't want to talk. We were women…we always wanted to talk. It was just the realization that this kind of emotion, so deep, so powerful, was sometimes beyond words. Sometimes words could get in the way of a moment like that, and none of us wanted anything to get in the middle of that hug. It was enough.

The rest of the afternoon did justice to Father's Day: red meat, competitive games, and two dads who smiled for hours. By the time the sunset colored the sky gold, red, and purple, we all had a deep feeling of satisfaction. We'd managed another family event that felt oddly wonderful and familiar. Yes, oddly. Because honestly, six months before, we didn't know for sure if we'd ever do those things again.

When there's a family crisis of this magnitude, "normal" and "routine" seem as elusive as stable ground in an earthquake. You just keep putting your foot down, hoping one day the ground will stop moving and you can start to rebuild all the wreckage.

Now that we'd been rebuilding for months, I was beginning to see structural outlines and concrete foundations, and somehow I knew we'd be all right. Our family would survive. In fact, I was beginning to think we might even become stronger.

« »

37

It was early June when I realized men were noticing me. I'd be walking down the sidewalk and get a lingering glance from some thirty-something businessman. Or I'd be in Java Jungle and catch a nice-looking guy taking a second look. Clearly exercise was reactivating my sexy.

I needed a boost in that department. I'd been kicking myself again, trying to figure out how I could have been dumb enough to let Austin slip away. I'd played out a few scenarios in my mind where I picked up the phone and called him, but each time I realized I couldn't get past "hello." I felt too badly about the way I'd treated him. He was a great guy who deserved better, so I never called. I just had to accept that Austin was my "superior man discarded." I consoled myself that most women had one, and accepted the fact he was probably one of very few superior men in this world, which meant I just had to get used to dating "average guy" again. It didn't seem very appealing...until men started noticing me.

Within a couple of weeks, one of those nice-looking guys was talking to me in line. By the end of the week I had a date for Saturday night and felt pretty secure in my attractiveness quotient.

Erick and I went out a few times. Great guy. Not enough in common for a long-term relationship. Then Jim and I went out a few times. Wonderful person, just not the right chemistry. We both felt it.

Jen and I were discussing all this one Sunday afternoon as we made dinner. I was spending a lot more time at Jen and Charlie's house, relishing my time with Blake and Sophie who were now old enough to play Mexican Train Dominos, one of my favorite games. The last time we'd played, it was

Blake and Jen against Sophie and me—a pretty even match even though Sophie and I were clearly the more devious pair. This particular Sunday afternoon Blake and Sophie were next door playing with the Townsend twins while Jen and I fixed dinner. Charlie was watching baseball, cheering for the Dodgers and deeply involved in Vin Scully's running commentary. Jen and I were talking about men—again.

"It's weird," I told Jen. "Guys seem to have this radar that picks up on a woman's feelings of attractiveness. When I feel sexy and confident, I get more looks than a Ferrari. If I'm already dating someone, I'm a guy magnet. But when I feel down or unenergetic, I can't get a look if I paid for it."

"Yeah, I remember that," Jen said. "Women must put off a confidence pheromone or something."

"I wonder how guys pick up on that?" I said. "It doesn't seem like women have that kind of radar. We'll go out with any loser who has a set of biceps."

"Sad but true." Jen laughed. It felt good to laugh with my sister. Her kitchen felt familiar and friendly again, a place for girlfriend talk and good advice.

"Hey, I know how we can make our millions," I said. "We need to develop a make-up that gives off the illusion of sexy self-confidence. Maybe even a glow that says, 'I have seven guys calling me already, so get in line.'"

"Isn't that what every make-up brand promises?" Jen asked as she launched into her best impression of a TV ad. "Wear Cover Girl and you will exude sexiness. It will seep out of your pores and grab the best man within a three-mile radius who will instantly become your sex slave for life." Jen quickly looked around. "The kids are still gone, aren't they?"

We both giggled. The Dodgers scored a run, and Charlie cheered. I went back to making carrot curls and dicing cucumber for the salad. "It does feel good to be dating again," I said. "My body looks better after all those miles of running, and my mind feels clearer."

"Clearer in what way?" Jen asked.

"I don't know...just more focused on the important things of life," I said. "After all our family's been through, I think we've all done some serious self-evaluation. I feel like I know myself better now. If I ever was superficial, I don't think I could ever be again."

"You were never superficial," Jen said, "but you were a little judgmental."

"Yeah, I know."

"And, just for the record," Jen said quickly, "I have noticed that you've softened. You've always had a confident air about you, but now it's there without the harshly opinionated edges."

"Was I harshly opinionated before?" I asked.

"Sometimes," Jen said gently. "Maybe just a little."

I looked deeply into the salad bowl. There wasn't anything special to see in there, but I still looked. It gave my eyes something to do while my brain digested Jen's words. "I guess none of us really know exactly how we come across," I said after a long pause.

"No, we really don't. That's why we have family. To keep us real," Jen said as she looked directly at me. "To keep us from believing our own press."

"It's a good thing," I said. "I guess if I want a clearly superior guy, I have to be a superior woman, and that requires self-examination."

"Such fun." Jen rolled her eyes.

We worked a little more on the chicken and the salad and listened to the final inning of the baseball game. The Dodgers were down by a run in the bottom of the ninth with one runner on second and two outs. The crowd noise accelerated. Vin Scully was reviewing the stats of the batter, who with any luck at all would get the winning hit.

I thought about all the weight on that one guy.

"So," Jen asked. "How are you doing in the dating department?"

"Not too bad," I said. "I've gone out with a couple nice guys. I'm just waiting for a little more chemistry and compatibility."

"It won't work if those are missing," Jen said matter-of-factly.

"Yeah, I know," I replied. "It's either there or it's not, which complicates the snot out of life." Just then Charlie walked into the kitchen and announced the Dodgers had won. Three months before just being in the same room with him would have made me nervous, but it didn't anymore.

"So did I hear you're dating someone?" Charlie asked.

"No one in particular," I responded. "Just dating."

"Well," Charlie said, "keep fishing. You've got the right bait to land a great guy."

I looked at Jen with a puzzled look. Jen leaned playfully against Charlie. "Great analogy, Shakespeare," Jen joked as she shook her head and rolled her eyes. "My baby sister doesn't need to do any fishing. She's the grand prize at the end of the tournament!"

"Yeah, right," I said. I was feigning humility on the outside, but inside I was astounded at Jen's words. The sister who was always trying to improve me suddenly wasn't. It felt good.

Another quote popped into my mind, one I'd heard in church.

"Before a diamond shows its brilliancy and prismatic colors it has to stand a good deal of cutting and smoothing."

I think the pastor had said this in the context of pain and suffering. I didn't think much of it at the time because frankly I hadn't experienced much suffering beyond three years of junior high. My life had been cushioned by my parents and pre-paved by my sister. I'd lived a nice American middle-class existence.

But the last months had required a good deal of cutting and smoothing. I'd been forced to face my own judgmentalism, my own capacity for irrational emotion, my own weaknesses. They'd stalked me until I couldn't outrun them then pinned me to the ground and forced me to fight. It wasn't a fight I wanted, but somehow I was stronger and better for the battle.

Charlie wandered back into the family room to turn off the TV, Jen started setting the table, and Blake and Sophie burst through the back door racing upstairs to wash their hands. I leaned against the kitchen counter and savored the sights and smells of this routine family dinner. I'd have missed all this if I'd refused to learn from our crisis. We'd still be searching for a strong connection if Mom and Dad hadn't worked so hard to keep our family together. Jen's life would be an open wound if Charlie had refused counseling or ignored the doctor's recommendations. Although we had no proof the future would be secure, at least we still had each other. We'd climbed the mountain together, and we'd survived.

As I looked around the table that evening, I realized Charlie, not through his arrogance but through his weakness, had taught me something important about becoming a diamond. I'd always thought my life was good because it was planned and smooth. I had considered myself great wife material because I had a conventional background and a stable family. But it wasn't true.

Stability without challenge creates fragile people. Comfort without work creates entitled people. I'd been more flimsy and entitled than I wanted to admit.

Charlie's brush with death had knocked me off my protected shelf and forced me to realize no one is entitled to a life of predictability and ease. We just have to learn to step up, face the polishing, and do the hard work to become diamonds.

≪ ≫

38

I'd been running for more than six months, keeping those endorphins flowing and my mind focused through the summer and into the cooler days of fall.

The summer had been wonderful as Jen and I spent more time together and found new ways to adapt to the changed reality. Charlie was back at work, and Jen's hours were flexible, so we took the kids to the beach and watched their summer sports in the late afternoons. We hooked up two hoses in the backyard and had water fights, oldest children against youngest. Sophie and I usually won because we had no compunction about cheating.

As I hung around Jen's house I began to enjoy talking with Charlie, asking about his day at work or the Dodgers' chances of getting to the World Series.

My opinion of Charlie had started at "egotistical boyfriend" then moved to "pseudo-intellectual husband." Now I began to view Charlie as three-dimensional. He no longer fit a two-word classification. He was complex, like a pie chart with small slices of "caring father" and "vulnerable male" nestled beside "periodically self-aggrandizing brother-in-law." I began to realize Charlie had good and bad traits just like all the rest of my family. The difference was, I'd always forgiven my family for their weaknesses. Now I was willing to forgive Charlie for his.

Jen was open to discussing anything. We'd spent many summer hours talking about the whys and what-ifs. She wasn't afraid of my questions. They were familiar to her—topics she'd already broached with Dr. Neval and realized they weren't fatal if verbalized. And slowly I began to realize

Charlie wouldn't break if I talked openly with him too. He'd faced depression and knew it intimately. He was the family expert, and I was still learning.

Throughout the summer, our family had spent many evenings at Dad and Mom's house, the five adults munching on something from Mom's kitchen while the kids played in the pool. Mom still relied on food as a way to connect us, and it worked.

The stability Mom and Dad had shown in the face of crisis made me appreciate them more. I'm sure they'd spent their own nights crying. They didn't deny their pain; they just didn't let it overflow and drown all of us. They did what they'd always done. They drew us together and loved us and fed us. They reminded us we were family no matter what, and somehow we made it through the summer.

Now the days were getting shorter and cooler, and I was enjoying my running even more. My body was firmer, and my happiness was more consistent. I felt sexier, so I'd cleaned out my underwear drawer and made a Victoria's Secret run. There's nothing like brand new lace under your clothes to make you feel delicious.

Running had become part of my routine, and I expected my particular run one day to be completely routine. Head out, run a few miles, and be back home in time for dinner. I wasn't looking for the well-placed rock, but it clearly had its eye on me. The moment my ankle turned, I knew I was in trouble. I rolled to the left, felt something in my ankle tear, and hit the ground a moment later—knees first then both elbows and both hands. Saved the face, thank goodness.

Within seconds, a car pulled over, and an older couple ran to my side, the woman clutching a box of Kleenex in her hand. I remember thinking, "Wait. Isn't this the part where a handsome guy comes to my rescue and we fall madly in love?" But then I looked down and saw blood all over my pants. They insisted on calling 9-1-1. I insisted I was fine and would prefer to have my sister take me to a minor emergency clinic. After a little negotiating, they allowed me to sit in their back seat next to Tillie, a large slobbering Red Setter, and they drove me home. I hobbled into the kitchen, grabbed an ice pack for my ankle, and called Jen.

Three hours, two x-rays, and one set of crutches later, I was at Jen's house with my ankle wrapped, my foot elevated, road rash goop on my elbows and knees, and lots of pain killer in my bloodstream. I spent the night in her guestroom and soon realized her family's schedule and my discomfort just didn't mesh. So the next day, I went home to try it on my own.

There's nothing like crutches to make you appreciate healthy ankles. By the third day, my hands ached and my underarms were raw. I couldn't find a decent way to sleep without the pain meds, but I felt drugged when I woke up. I'd managed to make it back to work after a couple of days, although it hurt to bend my elbows. The big trick was showering. I'd finally swallowed my pride and called Jen, who graciously came over and helped me wash my hair and dry off without falling.

I've never been a particularly good sickie, but this time I was truly miserable. Mom brought over homemade soup, Dad called to check on me, Max brought me lunch at my desk, and Jen helped me shower and bought my groceries. But I still felt like crap.

Thursday evening, day ten of the misery, I was finally starting to feel better. The scabs on my elbows were nearly gone, although the area was still a lovely shade of purple and green. I'd abandoned my crutches days before and was tentatively putting more and more weight on my ankle. Work went well that day, and I'd dropped onto the couch and turned on the TV the minute I came home. I was thinking about what I could scrounge for dinner when the phone rang. Without looking at the caller ID, I answered.

"Hi." I instantly recognized the voice. The smooth baritone, the concern. It was Austin.

"I just heard you're on crutches. How are you doing?"

"Hi," I said, trying not to sound too surprised or excited. "Um…I'm surviving. How did you hear?"

"Oh, I still go to that bakery where we met. Remember?" he asked.

"Sure," I said. "I still go there too sometimes."

Of course I did. I thought of Austin whenever I was within thirty feet of that bakery. Whenever I stood in line I always looked around to see if he happened to be there, but he never was.

"Well, the guy there said he'd seen you on crutches. So I thought I should call and see if you were okay."

"That's sweet of you," I said. "I'm doing all right—now that the crutches are gone and I can bend my elbows. You should have seen me on the pain meds. I was part Paris Hilton and part Three Stooges. It was not a pretty picture." Austin laughed. I'd always liked his laugh, and hearing it again made me miss him.

"So what are you doing now?" he asked.

"Just sitting here watching TV."

"Have you eaten yet?"

"Not yet."

"Well," he hesitated for a moment. "I'm not too far from your house. I could pick up some sushi and bring it over if you like."

I couldn't help myself. I started smiling like a ninth-grade girl. I was still dressed up from work. I knew my make-up looked good, even after a full day, and my house was clean. It didn't get much better than that on short notice. "That would be great," I said. "Sushi sounds really good."

Sushi sounded better than good. Sushi sounded perfect.

Austin was at the door fifteen minutes later with sushi in one hand and flowers in the other. I can't quite describe what it felt like to see him again. I was excited, but beyond that, I knew as soon as I saw his face that something incredible was happening. We were being offered the gift of a second chance. Even with my bruises, it felt like the best gift in the world.

We talked, we ate sushi, we laughed. When we finally kissed, it was sweet and familiar. He held my face in his hands for a moment then said, "I've missed you."

"I've missed you too." The words came out easily.

"Really?" Austin asked. "I wasn't sure."

I looked at him, this wonderful man who had risked tonight's call when I hadn't found the courage to call him in months. "Yes, I missed you," I said. "I didn't reach out because I didn't know how. I didn't know how to tell you it was my fault, and I'm so sorry. I'm truly sorry we ever broke up."

Austin took my face in his hands and kissed me. Sometime during that long and lovely kiss, I knew I had been given another chance with this guy. It was a sweet and comforting realization.

I'd always thought Austin was the guy who could reach the bar. He had so many things I valued: strength, compassion, intelligence, kindness. Maybe our relationship would survive the separation because during our time apart, these same traits were being developed within me. The bar I'd once used to judge men had become my own mirror.

146

We sat and talked and kissed for a few more minutes then Austin gathered the remnants of our dinner and took them to the kitchen. He kissed me good night and promised to call the next day. I stood near the window for a few moments, waiting for the sound of his footsteps on the sidewalk.

As I crawled into bed that night, I realized I'd learned a great lesson from Austin—caring and love are stronger than pain and distance. When you love someone, you might have to give them space. You may even have to let them go for a while. But if you really care about them and you believe they care about you, sometimes you just have to come back and risk everything to try again.

≪ ≫

39

Today I sat in the sunshine eating my lunch, thinking about Austin and the men I've known in my life. I know there are a lot of marketing people who make their living portraying men as clueless husbands, self-centered boyfriends, and inferior co-workers. I also know there are plenty of men in this world who fit those stereotypes. (Believe me, I've dated a few and worked with more.) But I have to tell you, I've learned a lot from men.

Since Austin reentered my world with take-out sushi and a willingness to start over, I've been immersed in lessons about love. They go beyond the love my Dad modeled or the good advice Andrew gave me, deeper than the skeletal knowledge I gathered from Dave and Max.

The love I share with Austin has been tested and strengthened by the realities of life. We've been together over a year now. During the last thirteen months we've tackled the challenges of a friend's funeral, underhanded politics at work, and a plumbing leak that flooded my condo. We've spent time with both our families and talked openly about their unique circumstances. As we've faced and worked through the emotions surrounding all these situations, we've started to recognize the difference between the loves of our past and the love we feel for each other.

Our love seems to be built on core values that provide strength and stability. It's a love that requests rather than demands; it's intimately aware of the other person's time, feelings, and needs. Our love finds joy in cherishing the simple pleasures and feels exhilaration in solving the complex problems. My parents would call what we have "mature love." I haven't put a title to it yet, but I'm continually impressed by its vitality.

Our day-to-day life has developed a nice rhythm. We run together, laugh a lot, and disagree without going for the jugular. We cook together in the evenings, opening the kitchen window of my condo to let the breeze in and the workday stress out. I never enjoyed cooking much before, but somehow as we chop vegetables and braise meat I feel my shoulders loosen up and I see the muscles in Austin's face relax. Usually we talk about our workdays, about weekend plans, about life. If dinner needs to bake, we put on music and pour a glass of wine then settle down into the contours of the sofa and end up moments later in each other's arms. The magnetism is impossible to ignore and too rich to waste.

We've started attending church periodically; we had a deep conversation about our spiritual beliefs and decided it might be worth exploring together. For us there's a noticeable difference between the church attendance of our childhoods and the spirituality of our own decision. Choosing a church together added another dimension to our already strong sense of connection.

It seems like every facet of our relationship—social, emotional, physical, and spiritual—has created a strong desire to explore, delve into the depths, and enjoy the synergy.

On the family front, I had the chance to meet Austin's mom and step-dad last month when they were in town for a wedding. I wouldn't say I was nervous...well, okay, maybe a little. But I didn't need to be. They seem really nice, and we found lots to talk about over dinner. I still haven't met his sisters, so Austin and I are planning a trip north sometime this summer.

Austin racked up both Dad and Charlie's seal of approval within seconds of my acknowledgement that we were back together. I can't prove it, but I think Dad breathed a sigh of relief when I told him. Mom smiled all evening. And just for the record, I didn't really request Charlie's approval, but he insisted on telling me what he saw as Austin's strengths. For a change, I didn't mind listening.

Max and Austin met early on and found they can hang out pretty well but don't really have that much in common. Austin is clearly in the settling down stage of life and Max remains in the transient stage, although I think he would like to move out of it but isn't sure how.

I still haven't found a fatal flaw in Austin. Yes, he likes watching sports a little too much, refuses to go to chick flicks with me, and he won't get rid of that pathetic old brown jacket that's barely holding together, but somehow those things don't matter much to me anymore. The combination of chemistry, affection, and respect that surrounds Austin and me is too intriguing to be bothered with superficiality. We have something I can't fully describe and never want to lose. I'd like to dissect it and discuss the details with Jen, but somehow I don't think it can be microscopically analyzed. It has to be experienced. It's a journey for two, and I've always been one to enjoy the journey.

So I just keep learning more and more about love from Austin. With any luck at all, I hope to learn a lot more from him in the next forty or fifty years.

≪ ≫

A free reader's guide is available on www.jenellhollett.com

Made in the USA
Charleston, SC
24 July 2012